"Why didn't you tell me?" she asked

Brent looked at the tears shimmering in her eyes.

She knows.

He felt relieved. The charade was over. He crossed over to her and took her hands. "I was going to," he confessed. "I really wanted to. But I didn't know where or how to start."

Maggi pulled her hands back. She couldn't think when he touched her, couldn't focus her mind. Her professional outrage at being strung along warred with the hurt she felt personally. She had been ready to let herself go, to love this man who looked so in need of loving, and all the time he was stringing her along, waiting to pay her back.

"I don't believe you," she said quietly. "I think all you want is revenge."

He paused for a long moment. Finally, he answered her. "Yes."

ABOUT THE AUTHOR

Marie Ferrarella first tried her hand at writing
when she was eleven, composing scripts
for her favorite TV show, *Bonanza*. Though
she was not published until twenty-two years
later, she has to date written more than
twenty novels, under various pseudonyms.
Marie, who also holds a Master's degree in
Shakespearian comedy, lives with her
husband and two children in California.

Books by Marie Ferrarella

HARLEQUIN AMERICAN ROMANCE
145—POCKETFUL OF RAINBOWS

HARLEQUIN INTRIGUE
writing as Marie Nicole
21—THICK AS THIEVES
30—CODE NAME: LOVE

These books may be available at your local bookseller.

Don't miss any of our special offers. Write to us at the
following address for information on our newest releases.

Harlequin Reader Service
901 Fuhrmann Blvd., P.O. Box 1397, Buffalo, NY 14240
Canadian address: P.O. Box 2800, Postal Station A,
5170 Yonge St., Willowdale, Ont. M2N 6J3

Pocketful
of Rainbows

MARIE FERRARELLA

Harlequin Books

TORONTO • NEW YORK • LONDON
AMSTERDAM • PARIS • SYDNEY • HAMBURG
STOCKHOLM • ATHENS • TOKYO • MILAN

To Nancy King Arp,
who always did all the things I just dreamed about

———————————◆———————————

Published April 1986

First printing February 1986

ISBN 0-373-16145-X

Chapter One

Maggi Cole was in trouble.

She had sensed it for some time now. She had been so busy with hundreds of details that her anxiety had been held at bay. Sort of like the old cliché, she thought—can't see the forest for the trees. Her desk was cluttered with notes, reminders, bills—all clamoring for her personal attention. She had long since forgotten the color of the blotter she knew lay somewhere underneath. The phone rang constantly. There was always someone on the other end with a problem that had to be attended to immediately.

Maggi lifted the phone from its cradle and placed it on top of a stack of papers. Rolling her chair back, she slid down slightly, and gingerly massaged her temples, hoping to ease the tension. At that moment, she no longer sensed that she was in trouble; she knew it.

Struggling back upright, Maggi swung her swivel chair around and faced the window directly behind her desk. She wished she could throw it open. She had been breathing this stuffy recycled nonsense now for seven months; maybe some fresh air would clear her head. Then she smiled to herself. Fresh air? In New York? At eleven in the morning? All she'd get would be a lungful of exhaust from the steady stream of midtown traffic below.

Maggi sighed. It was her own fault. She had come up with this charity extravaganza. No one else had come and put it into her lap saying, "Please, please handle this for us." She had done it. She had raised her hand, figuratively, and volunteered to leave her nice California home, claiming she could manage it all: produce the famous people, set up the theater, get the accommodations, create the format....

All your own fault, Maggi.

She turned around and saw Norman Everett standing in her doorway, his head slightly cocked, patiently waiting. "I heard that sigh all the way in the next office. That bad?"

"It ain't good, Norman," she told him.

The producer didn't wait for an invitation from his former protégé. Instead, he walked into the cluttered room, sidestepping a disorderly tower of scripts Maggi was considering.

Maggi leveled her eyes at the heavyset man she had known for over thirty years. She shook her head in despair and tossed a stack of bills she had been thumbing through into the air. They floated back to earth, some landing on her desk, some on the floor.

"How come," she wanted to know, "in the dozen or so movies where Mickey Rooney talked Judy Garland into putting on a show, all they needed was their enthusiasm? Suddenly, they were tap-dancing their little feet off, saving the farm, or the school, or whatever it was they were saving in that particular picture. Never once did they have to shell out a dime. Why weren't they hounded by vultures, too?'' She wasn't serious, but it would have been nice if this venture were just half as easy.

Norman laughed. ''They also didn't sweat or go to the bathroom in those days. Reality has come a long way since then.''

''Reality,'' Maggi said, shoving papers around, ''is killing me. God, I hate details!''

''But you handle them so well,'' Norman told her, beginning to roll down his shirtsleeves.

''That's right, flatter me, my ego needs a boost.''

''I'd say your ego needed a drink. C'mon,'' he said, ''I'm buying.''

''At eleven in the morning?'' she asked incredulously.

''Why not? We'll beat the lunch crowd. Of course,'' he added wryly, ''we might still run into the breakfast crowd.''

Maggi hung up the phone and followed him into the office. ''People drink their breakfasts out here, too, huh?'' Maggi asked, amused, as she leaned against the door frame and waited for Norman to get his jacket. She suddenly felt terribly weary. Maybe she didn't need a drink, but she certainly needed something, she told herself.

Norman's plaid jacket made him look even squarer than he already was. He took her arm and ushered her out. "They do if they have to come in on the subway."

"What do you know about subways? I've seen you take nothing but taxis ever since we got here," Maggi scoffed as they walked into the elevator.

One stubby finger reached around Maggi to press "1." "You forget, I'm a native. Subways are what sent me scrambling for the California sunshine in the first place."

"That, and your ex-wife's overdue alimony payments." Maggi playfully reminded him.

"Details, details." Norman waved a hamlike hand in the air.

"You said I was good at that."

"There is such a thing as overdoing it, you know."

They reached the street level and Norman swung open a door, allowing Maggi to step out of the dark passageway and into the dimly lit, subdued atmosphere of a theater at rest. Today was Monday and the MacKenzie Theater lay dormant until the following evening, when several dozen pairs of sprightly dancing feet would bring Broadway's newest hit musical to life at seven-thirty.

"I wish I could overdo the donations we've received for the show," Maggi told him. She was dejected, weary of cajoling and pleading for money; that part of her job took its toll more than the rest of it did. But then, the rest of it was rather fun for her. Producers didn't have to slave over a script, trying to get it letter-perfect, but she enjoyed that; it kept her hand in the creative aspect of the entertainment industry.

The April air was heavy and damp as they walked out of the building. It felt as if it was just moments away from another annoying sprinkle. It had been drizzling off and on now for three days. The weather added nothing to her spirits, which were at the lowest point they had been since... well, since she couldn't remember when. Maggi hated failing. More than that, she hated letting people down. And there were so many people involved in this charity benefit now.

Briskly they walked down the block toward a coffee shop. Maggi hardly noticed the foot traffic as she became more and more submerged in her thoughts.

"Carpet's wearing thin already," Norman commented, looking down at the long red carpet beneath his feet. Six hundred square yards of royal red carpet had been set down in the street, creating a bright path from the MacKenzie Theater to the Amsterdam Hotel, where all the greats and neargreats Maggi had coerced into working on the benefit would be staying.

Norman's words roused Maggi out of her mental fog. "They promised it would last until after the performance—if there is a performance." It was exactly two and a half weeks away. How was she ever going to raise the money in time?

"I'm worried, Maggi," Norman said as they walked into the coffee shop.

"So am I."

The warm atmosphere felt good for a moment, it took the morning chill out of her bones. Then, just like the office, it began to feel oppressive. Nothing, Maggi decided, would satisfy her today. It was going to be one of those days. She knew it would be when she woke up this morning. Her carefree hairdo had suddenly demanded some care on her part. The shoulder-length, copper-gold hair began to frizz, conquered by the misty weather.

"I don't mean about the show," Norman told her, holding up two fingers in answer to the waitress's quizzical look. They were led to a booth by the window where they could look out on the avenue and watch the world go by. And be watched by the world as they ate, Maggi thought dryly. "I mean, I've never seen *you* so down and out before—not even when Alfred Lorenzo told you your contract with the studio was terminated."

Alfred Lorenzo. The name took her back a long way—twenty-two years to be exact. She was known as Maggi McCree then—the dancing, singing darling of the silver screen. But puberty had signaled an end to her days as a child star. She tried to recall her feelings on that day as she had stood in the studio head's ultraplush office, listening to the words that sent her into the realm of has-been child stars. She had experienced the stabbing pain of disappointment—acting was all she had ever known—but there had been a certain amount of relief as well. The charade was over. She had known, at thirteen, that she was hanging on by a thread. She was too old to be playing the roles the studio kept giving her, and she just wasn't exceptional enough to make the transition to adult parts. There weren't any parts for a thirteen-year-old, gangly girl who looked thirteen. She needed time to get over her awkward stage. Everything in those days was out of proportion. By the time it got back into proportion, she had been out of movies for four years, no longer hot, no longer in demand.

She remembered the day she had realized that Maggi McCree belonged to the past. She was seventeen and money was very, very tight for her and her mother. She had gone to her old studio and requested "an audience" with the new president. Lorenzo was gone and the new head of the studio "didn't have time for has-beens," his secretary had tersely told her. No one did. It was the same story everywhere she went.

Try as she might, Maggi couldn't divorce herself from the entertainment world. Life outside was just too dull in comparison. She had missed the world of filmmaking, missed the excitement of creating fantasy. So she turned to Norman, who had been her director on several movies and had treated her as if he were her father. Or what she had surmised a father was like, since her own had left her mother when Maggi was less than two years old.

Norman had taken her on as a script girl. Then, when he became a producer, she graduated to reading properties for him. She proved to have an excellent eye for picking box office smashes, so when Norman broke away from the studio and formed his own production company, he took Maggi with him. It turned out to be an opportune move for her. Her husband of less than four years had been killed in a freak auto accident, leaving her with two baby daughters, barely eleven months apart, and next to nothing else. Maggi's mother had long since mismanaged all the money Maggi had earned during her career.

Over the past fourteen years, their roles had gradually reversed, with Norman giving Maggi more and more responsibilities until it was Maggi who found herself calling the shots, with Norman backing her up, acting as her ever-faithful second string. Maggi had turned into a dynamo, a producer par excellence. She gained far more respect for herself in this capacity than she ever had as a child star. She was recognized as a power to be reckoned with, a person who delivered, someone with a great track record.

Until now.

"When Lorenzo fired me," Maggi said bluntly, toying with the beige menu the waitress had given her, "I had only myself and my mother to support. There weren't countless people depending on me as there are now. As of this moment, the cupboard is about to be declared bare and I don't know where my dog's next bone is coming from." She sighed wearily. "Coffee," she absently told the waitress who hovered next to her expectantly. "And a sweet roll."

The waitress looked at her blankly, her pencil halted in midscribble. "Sweet roll?" she echoed.

"She means a Danish," Norman clarified, surrendering his own menu. "You gotta forgive her. She's a foreigner," he explained. That seemed to satisfy the woman. Maggi hid her amusement as Norman ordered the same thing and the waitress shuffled off. "As to your 'dog' Mother Hubbard," Norman went on, turning his attention back to Maggi, "we'll get him a bone on credit."

"Credit's been stretched to the limit, Norman," Maggi said, absently looking out the window.

"Hey, there's Laura Lerner!" someone shouted, recognizing the nubile starlet of several fair-to-passing movies and a handful of sexy blue-jean ads. Several people turned to gape, including Maggi, who attempted a nonchalant glance in the woman's direction.

Norman tried to read her mind. "Miss those days, Maggi?" he asked. Someone stopped the starlet on the street and shoved a piece of paper and a pen into her hands.

"Not a whit," Maggi assured him, perhaps a little too quickly. "I like my private life."

"Sure you do," he muttered. "That's why you gave it up, leaving your family and friends to work on the East Coast. How many times have you seen Nikki and Rachel in the past seven months?"

She thought of her daughters and felt a pang of guilt. She missed them. There never seemed to be enough time to spend with them. Of all the things she had accomplished, she was proudest of the way they had turned out. *Probably despite you instead of because of you,* she thought. "Not nearly enough," Maggi sighed heavily, running her hand through her coppery hair. "Wonder how they're going to like having a failure as a mother."

The waitress returned with their order. As she set the coffees down, her attention was snared by the commotion at the window, and she looked out to see what was causing it. Maggi grabbed the waitress's hand as she saw her Danish sliding off the plate, aimed straight for her lap. The waitress gave her a contrite look, then retreated.

"You're not a failure; something will come through." Norman assured Maggi. His round face looked the picture of confidence.

"If you break into one of those sickeningly sweet songs I used to sing in those god-awful musicals, I'll kick you," Maggi threatened.

Norman held up his hands in defense. "No happy song—even though you've found more silver linings than anyone else I've ever known."

"Until now," Maggi took a bite out of the Danish and pieces of the sugar coating fell back onto her plate. "All right, who haven't we hit up for money?" she asked.

"God. Three monks in Tibet. And the little old lady from Pasadena," Norman told her, ticking each off on his fingers. He took a sip of his coffee and made a face.

"Not strong enough?" She knew Norman liked his coffee to be able to support his spoon in an upright position. He shook his head in reply. "Who else?" Maggi pressed.

"My mother".

"You haven't got a mother, Norman. You stepped out of Lorenzo's head, fully grown, like Athena out of Zeus's head. At least that's what you've always told me."

He nodded. "Right, I forgot. All this exhaust makes me forget things. Can't wait to get back to L.A.," he said longingly.

"And L.A. smog?" she teased.

"I've gotten used to it." He shrugged.

So had she, she thought. Actually, California was all she had ever known, and she loved it. She loved the almost constant sunshine and the fact that the rain didn't dare fall except in the prescribed months. *Like Camelot,* she thought with a fond smile. She noticed Norman looking at her oddly and turned her mind back to business. "Who else is there, really?"

Norman became more serious as he considered her question. "There's the Wallaby Medical Research Foundation," he said finally.

"Why haven't we asked them?" Maggi asked, taking a sip of her coffee. One taste told her that Norman was right. Someone must have substituted dishwater in the coffee urn. She pushed the cup aside and looked expectantly at Norman's jowly face. Norman had come up with the original list of donors they could approach for financial support.

"Because the board's conservative," he explained.

"That's no reason," Maggi commented. "We're not exactly raising money to overthrow the government."

"And the top administrator of the foundation is a stuffed shirt—"

"So? We'll unstuff him," Maggi said with nascent enthusiasm.

"Word has it that he hates the performing arts. And since this benefit is supposed to help renovate the ac-

tors' retirement home and hospital..." His voice
trailed off, sounding a note of hopelessness.

"Ah, a challenge!" Maggi brightened, a smile beginning to spread across her delicate, china-doll features. When Maggi looked serious, her face looked to
Norman like that of a high-class, reserved beauty, but
when she smiled, there was something definitely pix-
ieish in her expression. It was that look he saw now.

"More than a challenge," he told her. "It's damn
near impossible to get to see him."

"Have you tried?"

"Three times. Man's in, but never to us. I couldn't
even get past the guard at the security desk."

"Security desk?" Maggi echoed, surprised.

Norman nodded. "He's walled up tighter than the
princess in the tower." Norman was making a joking
reference to the last movie Maggi had appeared in. It
was based on *Rapunzel*. It was also dreadful.

"We'll get him to let his hair down so that I can
climb the golden stair."

Norman shook his head. "If you can get in to see
him, I'll believe you can walk on water."

"In New York, I probably can," Maggi quipped.
"At least across the East River. C'mon," she urged,
rising.

Norman wrapped his half-eaten Danish in a napkin, then stuffed it into his jacket as he got up.
"Where to?"

"Back to the office," she answered, already three
steps ahead of him. "I've got work to do."

After a second's hesitation, Norman picked up Maggi's Danish as well and threw down a five-dollar bill. He hurried after her, still nibbling.

IT WAS HIS VOICE that appealed to her at first. Deep and resonant, it was the kind of voice that one would expect of a trained Shakespearean actor.

"What the hell are you doing here?"

Of course, that wasn't the kind of thing one usually heard uttered by a Shakespearean actor, but under the circumstances, she couldn't quite blame him. After all, she had managed to breach his inner sanctum—something, she wagered, no one else had done, at least not lately.

Brent Sommerfield looked like the picture of the well-bred, well-schooled executive. She bet even his pajamas came in three-piece sets. He was impeccably dressed in a navy-blue three-piece suit with a light blue shirt and a dark blue tie. A streak of gray was beginning to touch his temples lovingly, accenting his dark hair. He had a commanding air about him and Maggi had no doubt that the imposing, six-foot-tall man probably struck fear into the hearts of his subordinates.

But Maggi had grown up working with some of the reigning terrors of Hollywood, directors who made their wishes known by roared mandates. Compared to them, Brent Sommerfield was a pussycat. Compared to them, he was also incredibly good-looking, even if his Roman nose could have been just a touch smaller.

The steel-blue eyes narrowed as he looked at Maggi, sitting comfortably next to his philodendron. Someone else, she judged, might have jumped three feet into the air if he had come into his office, expecting to find it empty, only to discover her sitting there. But Brent regarded her with half interest and half annoyance. She wondered which half would win out.

"I've come to talk to you about a matter of great importance," Maggi said, not rising from her seat. She knew what an impressive image she presented. Norman had told her that she had the best legs he'd ever seen, and she kept them crossed before her now, the long slit in her pale green skirt provocatively emphasizing them for Brent's viewing pleasure. Maggi hadn't been around the dreammakers for nothing; she had learned a few things. One of which was that it never hurt to put your best asset forward when trying to convince someone to do something he had no intention of doing. Such as investing in a charity benefit.

"How did you get in here?" he wanted to know, his brow furrowing in perplexity as he studied her. Studied her well, Maggi thought, watching his eyes as he drew nearer.

"It wasn't easy," she confessed readily.

It hadn't been. She had arrived at the front door, to be scrutinized by a giant of a man who acted as the security guard and looked like a lineman on an all-star football team. She had acted indignant when he couldn't find her name on his list of people who had appointments with Brent Sommerfield that day, so indignant that he had called his superior to check out her story.

While the burly man's back was turned, Maggi had slipped into the elevator and made her way up to Sommerfield's suite of offices.

There, a secretary who looked as if she had been sitting at her desk ever since time began regarded Maggi suspiciously over the top of her bifocals when Maggi insisted that she had an appointment.

"I make all of Mr. Sommerfield's appointments," the woman informed her haughtily.

Maggi began to grow angry. "Look, all I know is I called, spoke to someone named Miss Callahan, and she told me to come in today at one. Why can't you people run things more efficiently?" she demanded, putting her hands on her hips.

"Callahan?" the woman repeated, appearing to back down a trifle.

"Callahan," Maggi confirmed. "At one."

"Maybe that was when I left my desk for a few minutes on Thursday..." The woman looked at Maggi, waiting.

"I called on Friday," Maggi told her, not falling for the obvious trap.

It befuddled the woman, Maggi noted triumphantly. The granite pose gave way slightly as the older woman bit the inside of her lower lip and sucked it in. "Maybe I did leave my desk..." She was almost willing to concede. She looked up sharply. "Was it lunchtime?"

"Perhaps yours," Maggi said vaguely. "I haven't had time for lunch lately." She added the proper vexed tones to her voice.

The woman sighed in annoyance. "Must have been that new woman from the tenth floor. Can't send me anyone decent, can they?" she muttered to herself.

"I wouldn't know," Maggi said coldly, enjoying herself to the hilt. *It's the ham in you, Maggi.* "All I know is that I have an appointment and time is growing short for me." She glanced at her watch impatiently.

The secretary looked down at her desk calendar. "Well, I might be able to squeeze you in," she said, reconsidering. "Wait here. I have to check something." She marched down the hall like a soldier in training.

Maggi had no intention of "waiting here." As soon as the woman had turned the corner, Maggi darted down the hall. This was silly, she thought, playing hide-and-seek at her age. Where was the dignity? she asked herself. Then a smile curved her lips as she caught sight of her goal. Where was the fun otherwise? She stealthily made her way to the opaque glass door with the gold lettering proclaiming the office belonged to Brent Sommerfield, Chief Administrator.

The door was unlocked and the office unoccupied. Maggi sank down into the first chair that was off to the side. She didn't want him to see her as soon as he came in. As she waited, she went over what she wanted to say to him.

But she found herself unprepared when he finally came in, and consequently, Brent Sommerfield was able to get out the first words that signaled their initial confrontation.

As she looked at him now, Maggi found herself smiling despite the displeasure evident in his words. Her strategy was quickly being revamped in light of this newest piece of important information: The man was gorgeous.

Chapter Two

Maggi opened her mouth to speak. Just then, the door swung open and the secretary marched in, glaring at her accusingly.

"I thought you'd be here." The statement dripped with venom. "Mr. Sommerfield, I'm so sorry. She managed to—"

"Yes, she did, didn't she?" Brent said. Amusement flashed through his eyes and spread to his lips. Without his saying a word, Maggi could see that he looked intrigued by her ingenuity, despite his annoyance. "That's all right, Marietta. I can handle it from here."

Marietta? Yes, the name fit her, Maggi thought. The woman looked as if she were from a bygone era. Maggi half expected to see a bustle when the woman huffily turned her back.

"Well," Marietta said slowly, obviously not convinced that she should leave her employer with the likes of Maggi, "if you think it's all right . . . But I can send for Taylor,'' she added briskly, shooting Maggi a glare over her shoulder.

''Taylor obviously didn't do us any good at his post downstairs, did he?'' Brent pointed out, dismissing the suggestion. Marietta looked disappointed.

Taylor, Maggi surmised, must have been the guard she had hoodwinked. She knew he'd be none too happy to see her and was relieved Brent wasn't sending for him.

Despite the situation and the urgency of her mission, Maggi found her mind wandering. As she admired the appealing man standing before her, her thoughts had little to do with business. Tall, dark and handsome—wasn't that the old line? Well, he certainly filled it better than she had ever seen it filled.

As he drew nearer. the only lines Maggi saw were the two bordering the sides of his mouth. Were they laugh lines, she wondered, or frown lines? Norman had called him a stuffed shirt. Probably frown lines, if Norman was right in his assessment—and he usually was. But something within Maggi hoped that just this once he was wrong. She felt an attraction stir within her and tried to dismiss it. This was a hell of a time to be entertaining that kind of thought.

''It's all right, Marietta,'' Brent repeated, emphasizing the words.

Slowly, the bespectacled, angular creature in the tan business suit retreated, giving Maggi a warning look.

Maggi flashed Brent a smile. She could sense that she was being appraised—subtly, but nonetheless, appraised. She hoped he liked what he saw. Anything to get him to lend a friendly ear to her cause.

He leaned against the back of his desk, crossing his arms before his chest. "Well, you're too pretty to be a cat burglar; at least, you're not dressed for it. How did you get past Taylor and Marietta?" he wanted to know.

"Luck, and a little fancy footwork," she told him honestly.

He nodded, then his eyes narrowed just a little. "And what is it you want from me?"

"Just a little of your time," Maggi said, feeling it prudent to proceed with caution. Blurting out that she wanted his foundation's financial assistance backing to the tune of perhaps a quarter of a million dollars didn't quite seem the way to go at the moment.

"A little is all I have right now," he told her. "I have to be at a meeting in the Wall Street area in an hour." He glanced at his watch. "You have five minutes."

That wasn't nearly enough time. It might have been if she were approaching a genial donor, but Norman had said that Brent didn't care for the performing arts. Maggi knew that as soon as she told him what she was doing here, he would tune her out.

"I'm going to need more than that," she told him.

He looked intrigued. "Indeed?"

She hadn't heard that word used in a long time, not in that tone. He *was* a bit stuffy, despite his smile, she thought.

She considered asking if she could accompany him on his way to Wall Street, but decided against it. His mind would be preoccupied with the details of the meeting and Maggi wouldn't settle for anything less than his full attention.

"How about dinner?" she proposed suddenly.

He looked taken aback, and then amused. "I'm used to doing the asking," he said.

Yes, she was sure he was. Women's liberation was probably nothing more than a minor annoyance to him. Undoubtedly a chauvinist as well, she judged. Lord, this was getting tougher by the minute.

"I'm afraid I can't stand on ceremony," Maggi said. "What I have to talk to you about is very important and needs more than five minutes of your time."

"Four minutes," he corrected, glancing at his watch again.

She wondered if he was the type to make little mental lists for himself, and then stick to them. He looked as if he throve on schedules and was maddeningly efficient.

"Four minutes," she repeated. "What would you say if I picked you up here at, say, five-thirty?"

"I'd say you'd be standing around by yourself for a long time," he answered. "I don't expect to be back until at least six."

"Six, then," she amended, not about to be put off.

"And you won't tell me what this is all about?" he prodded. He looked, to Maggi's satisfaction, rather interested; the annoyed look he had worn at the outset was completely gone.

"Not yet," she replied, smiling.

"Ah, a woman of mystery." The corners of his mouth rose, highlighting high cheekbones. Then the smile fell a bit as his brows narrowed once more, almost meeting over the bridge of his nose. "This wouldn't be some sort of a terrorist plot, would it?"

Maggi tried to determine if he was joking. High-placed industrialists did run the risk of being taken prisoner by terrorist groups, but that was in foreign countries, not here. Was this something he lived with, this fear? "You can search me for weapons if you like," she offered glibly.

What had come over her? she asked herself. She was flirting unabashedly with the man. What was she planning to do, seduce him for the money? Well, that wouldn't be the worst way to go.... She skidded to a halt. What was going on here? Was it just overwork? She hadn't reacted to a man in this manner since before Johnny had died.

Maggi studied Brent's face for a reaction to her words, biting her lower lip and hoping she hadn't gone too far. She half expected a cold, flinty look to overtake his gaze. No such look came. "Now that sounds intriguing," Brent mused aloud.

The intercom buzzer sounded, demanding immediate attention. Brent disregarded it, staring straight into Maggi's eyes. She unfolded her legs slowly, stood up and walked deliberately toward him, stopping only a few inches away. The buzzer sounded more urgently. Maggi could actually feel the electricity crackle between them.

"Will you have dinner with me?" Maggi pressed again. "At a restaurant of your choice?" she added, hoping that would erase any doubts he might have.

"I don't care for restaurant food. How about my apartment?"

She hadn't expected that, and hesitated for a moment. He had neatly turned the tables on her. She saw the challenge in Brent's eyes, a look that seemed to mock her just a little. Maggi drew herself up to her five-foot-two stature, though she still, despite her three-inch heels, appeared tiny in comparison to his well-proportioned frame.

"You seem uncertain. You could search me for weapons, too, if you'd like. As a matter of fact, that might be an interesting way to start the evening."

Was he being sarcastic, or just playful? She couldn't quite tell.

"Done," Maggi said. If there was no other way, she would have to beard the lion in his den—or was she a fly stepping into the spider's parlor? No, she was an adult who could handle any given situation. After all, the man was a respected, well-known executive. There was nothing to be afraid of, except failure.

The intercom squawked again, but still went ignored. "Fine," he told Maggi. "If you get there before I do, Saunders will make you comfortable."

"Saunders?"

"My valet."

"Of course." A valet was far more his style than a housekeeper, even though Maggi thought valets had gone out with drawing-room comedies.

As she made a move to leave, Brent reached out and took hold of her wrist. His fleeting touch generated an inexplicable warmth through Maggi that spread quickly from her wrist to her extremeties. Yes, there was definitely a spark dancing between them, Maggi thought. She was going to have to proceed with caution.

"It might help if you had a name," Brent said.

Her name. How stupid of her. She had been so involved with the logistics of this escapade that she hadn't even given him her name.

"Maggi Cole." She watched his face for a sign of recognition. Except for a tightening of his jaw, there was none. Obviously, he either hadn't paid any attention to Norman's three entreaties to gain an audience with him, or Norman hadn't mentioned her name to the secretary in connection with their cause. In either case, her name appeared to mean nothing to him. So much the better for now, she decided. She didn't want him prejudiced before she got started.

The buzzer ceased its high-pitched demands abruptly, dying in midsquawk. In its place came a determined knock on the door. Brent's eyes were still on Maggi's face.

What was he thinking? she wondered. The blue pools were unfathomable.

The door swung open quickly. "Mr. Sommerfield, you'll be late for your meeting," Marietta reminded him, scowling at Maggi.

"Yes," he agreed. He picked up his briefcase and headed for the door. Then he stopped. He took a card from his pocket, scribbled something on the back, then handed it to Maggi.

It was hardly a scribble, she thought, glancing down at the card. The pencil lettering was almost perfect. It figured.

"That's my home address," he told her. His manner indicated that he expected her to leave the office with him, so Maggi fell into step.

Marietta's small eyes grew into slits as Maggi passed her.

"Does she always guard you like that?" Maggi asked as they approached the elevator.

"Marietta's invaluable," Brent informed her. There was a note of affection evident in his voice.

"Yes," Maggi agreed noncommittally, "but is she human?"

She was certain Marietta heard her as the elevator doors closed.

"YOU GOT AN AUDIENCE with His Holiness?" Norman asked incredulously, watching Maggi sit down in her chair. She nodded, confirming her statement. Norman scratched his head in awe, setting the thinning wisps of hair at attention. "Sometimes you amaze me. I don't know how you do it," he marveled.

"I haven't done it yet," she reminded him. "Seeing him is one thing, getting him to part with the foundation's money is quite another." She had traded places with Norman: Now it was Maggi who was uncertain about the venture while Norman glowed with confidence.

He dragged a chair over to Maggi's desk and straddled it as he looked at her eagerly. "What was he like?"

"Just as you said," Maggi answered. "He's a stuffed shirt. A tall, extremely attractive stuffed shirt, but one nonetheless."

"So? Unstuff him. Those were your intentions," he reminded her.

"Easier said than done, Norman," Maggi sighed. In her mind's eye, she saw the determined set of Sommerfield's square chin. There was a Missouri show-me attitude beneath that smooth exterior. He wasn't going to be swayed easily, not by a long shot.

"If anyone can do it," Norman countered enthusiastically, "you can, Maggi. Anything short of feeding the masses with five loaves and three fishes—my money's on you."

Maggi laughed. "Boy, you sure can lay it on thick."

The shaggy, wayward brows rose. "Is there any other way?" he asked innocently. Then he became more serious. "Are you sure you'll be all right, going up to see him in his apartment?"

"I'm thirty-five years old, Norman. Hardly a virginal maiden to be taken advantage of." For dramatic effect, she put her hand to her forehead and rolled her eyes upward.

"You're not exactly Old Paint, either," Norman pointed out. "You're a damn attractive woman and if I hadn't practically diapered you, I'd be after you myself."

Maggi reached out and touched his cheek fondly, "Thank you, Norman, I needed that." The phone started to ring again and she fought an urge to rip the cord out of the wall. For seven months she had listened to this phone, so that she now had a constant ringing in her ears. "Besides, the man has a valet," she went on, ignoring the sound. "How dangerous could he be with a valet?"

"Dr. Jekyll had one."

"That's fiction—and besides, he had a housekeeper. She probably mothered him to death. Brent Sommerfield didn't have a mother. Some corporate executive planned him on the drawing board and then had him assembled. And they sure put the parts together well." She grinned, a twinkle entering her eyes.

Norman studied her in silence for a moment. "Just what do these plans look like?"

Maggi put her hand on the telephone receiver, willing it to be silent. "If you were still in the business of casting movies, you'd want him for your leading man every time. *Filmplay Magazine* would run him on the cover every other month," she guaranteed. "Maybe every month," she amended.

"That good-looking?"

"That good-looking."

"Watch yourself, Maggi," he warned.

She looked at him curiously, surprised at his concern. "Why? I'm not exactly given to falling for good-looking men."

"That's exactly what I mean," Norman said, rising and going toward the door. His foot hit a tall stack of scripts. The column wavered for a moment, then toppled. Maggi was quick to join him on the floor, setting the pile back in its original haphazard order. Anything to ignore the telephone.

"Just what exactly *do* you mean?" she wanted to know.

He shrugged. "You've got a funny look in your eyes—"

"They're bloodshot," she insisted.

"No," he said, shaking his head. "That's something else. I think he's whet your appetite."

"I've had no appetite since Johnny died," she said, her voice serious.

She hadn't, really. Over the past fourteen years, she had gone out with a great many men and the evenings were almost always pleasant. But there had never been that same spark she had felt when she was with Johnny. Maybe, she had begun to think, that spark had only been there because she was seventeen when she fell in love with him and he had been so special to her. Johnny had been a bit player in B movies, and she had met him on the set of one of Norman's pictures. She remembered thinking then that he was destined for the top. He had been too good-looking and appealing not to have attracted a strong following. He had certainly snatched her heart away after only a few minutes. Norman had acted as Cupid, engineering their first date. It was all the push that was necessary. She and Johnny were married within two months. From white to black in four years, she thought ruefully. After his death, she threw herself headlong into her work and caring for her daughters. That was all there had been for all these years.

"It's not natural, Maggi," Norman declared, shaking his head. "It's just not natural."

"You've already said that," she told him, propping the stack of scripts against the leg of a chair and hoping that would do the trick until she got around to reading them. She felt overwhelmed by the work to do.

"Bears repeating," Norman said, turning to look at her once more, his hands hovering over the doorknob. "Women like you save it all up and then one day—whoosh, it all explodes."

"I'll try not to explode until the show's over," she promised, rising to her feet and brushing the wrinkles out of her skirt.

"Make jokes if you want to, but I've seen it happen time and again."

"Norman," Maggi said wearily.

"Yes?"

"Go to your office and answer the phone for me."

"Changing the subject won't do you any good," Norman pointed out, refusing to be put off.

"No, but getting you to answer the phone will." She took a deep breath and made a decision. "I am going out."

"Again?"

"I need to unwind a little before I lock horns with the illustrious Mr. Sommerfield. Where's the nearest health spa?" she asked. Norman kept a list of all the available conveniences so they could fill whatever request any of the incoming stars might have.

He scratched his head and thought a minute before giving her an address. "Plan on working out your tension?" He gave her a knowing look.

"No, Norman, I plan on sweating it out," she said as she picked up her purse and joined him in the doorway.

"Come again?"

"I want to sit in a steam room and let every pore in my body relax." The shrill ringing seemed to be getting louder. She looked back at the culprit on her desk. Now three lines were lit. Where *was* that secretary they had hired from the temporary agency? "Norman—"

He held his hand up. "I know, I know. Answer the phone." He retreated behind his own door.

Maggi looked after him affectionately. Where would she be without Norman? Probably selling matches in the snow, he had once laughingly told her. He wouldn't have been far from wrong. She had been pretty much beside herself when Johnny died. Norman was the one who had taken over, set her straight, given her someone to lean on until she got her bearings. Norman had been her center of calm in the midst of the storm around her.

Even now he should have been retired, basking in the peace and serenity his long years as a producer had earned him. He had talked about becoming a silent partner in the firm he had started, easing control over in her direction. But he stayed on because she needed him, capable though she was. She still needed him and his boundless friendship. Norman, she knew, was definitely one of a kind.

And so, Maggi thought, was Brent Sommerfield. His vivid, handsome profile flashed through her mind's eye as she walked to the elevator. She was going to need all her faculties well honed in order to convince him. She wasn't going to be up to par feeling this beat.

She hailed a cab and gave the driver the spa's address.

THE CLUB WAS FOR MEMBERS only and Maggi found herself agreeing to give the spa a "trial run." At this point, she was willing to sign half her soul away. There was something almost mystically medicinal about the vapors that rose up around her from the steam room. The nubile woman who tendered the trial subscription looked fairly disappointed that Maggi didn't want to rush right in and participate in their aerobics class.

"Not unless you want a corpse on your hands," Maggi told her.

"It'll get your blood moving," the wispy-looking woman said enthusiastically.

"Tomorrow—it'll move tomorrow," Maggi promised. "Today, it just wants to sit there. Trust me, I know my own blood."

The woman shrugged, obviously displeased at Maggi's determination to avoid physical exercise. Normally Maggi was very active physically, in fact, when she was back home, there had always been time for a tennis game or two, usually against one of her daughters. Raised on the game, they could now be counted on to give her a run for her money. But that was back there. Here, lately, her exercise consisted of lifting the telephone, listening to some complaint and trying to rectify the situation. That didn't tone muscles, but it certainly did weary the soul.

"Where's your steam room?" she asked again.

"Right through there." The woman pointed toward the far end of the corridor.

Maggi found her own way, passing a room filled to capacity with enthusiastic, jumping bodies of all sizes and shapes. The room was mirrored on three sides to emphasize all the participants' shortcomings. Maggi sighed and went on.

She stripped off her clothes in the locker room and wrapped herself in a large, downy white towel. Opening the heavy door leading into the steam room, Maggi felt as if she had walked into a scene out of Dante's *Inferno*. Guests of the spa were scattered throughout the room, mummified in sheets or towels and lying about in wilted poses.

Thick clouds of steam rose around Maggi as she made her way to an uninhabited wooden bench. She leaned her shoulders against the raised step behind her, closed her eyes and sighed deeply.

Relax. I've got to relax, she told herself.

Soon, her body felt utterly languid. It was as if she hadn't the strength or desire to move a muscle. This wasn't going to do, either, she told herself. The thought moved in slow motion through her brain. She didn't want to fall asleep when she saw Sommerfield. She wanted to be vital, alive, not something he could pour into a soup bowl. A good massage should do the trick, she decided. Was there one to be had around here?

With considerable effort, she rose and walked over to another tenant of the steam room. The reed-thin woman looked as if she would disappear completely if one more ounce of water was allowed to leave her body.

"Um, excuse me," Maggi tapped the woman's bony shoulder. One critical eye opened in Maggi's direction. The woman looked more than a little annoyed at being disturbed. "Do they have a masseuse available?"

"Helga's around if you're into torture," came the reply through bloodless lips.

Helga. Of course. What else would a masseuse be called? Except, maybe, Bruno. "Where can I find Helga?" Might as well be brave.

An irritated sigh escaped through flared nostrils. "That door, there." A twiglike finger pointed off into the opposite direction.

"Thank you," Maggi muttered and parted the fog as she moved toward the door. When she opened it, an amiable, heavyset woman sitting in the corner looked up from her magazine. Helga no doubt. For a moment, Maggi had second thoughts about her request, then shrugged.

"I'd like a massage."

The woman was on her feet instantly. She towered over Maggi. "Wonderful." Helga reached for the liniment, patting the table with one massive hand.

As Maggi pulled herself onto the table, she wondered if all those actors and actresses who frequented the retirement home and hospital that her benefit show hoped to refurbish were going to appreciate the sacrifice she was about to make.

Chapter Three

By all rights, Brent should have felt elated. He had just succeeded in getting the head of Skyways Airlines to pledge a three-million-dollar donation over the the next two years. That would go a long way toward providing Alhambra Medical School with the necessary research equipment they had petitioned for, not to mention tying up a few loose ends in a few other corners.

Normally, Brent found his work for the foundation very satisfying. Although he did not consider himself the gregarious sort, certainly not in his brother's league, he did rather well as the foundation's chief public relations man. In his own smooth, quiet manner, he managed to win the ear of many a busy top executive.

But today Brent's mind wasn't on his work, or on his triumph. It was on Maggi, and on his brother—his late brother. Emotions he had long thought dead flooded him, emotions he was not comfortable with, emotions that were tied to the person he used to be before he had worked himself up to a success.

That shy, tortured boy came back now, came back with his mother's harsh words ringing in his ears.

"She's responsible for all this. Remember that, Brent. *She* did this to us."

Maggi Cole, Brent thought, rolling the name around in his mind as his chauffeur carefully maneuvered the Bentley through the teeming downtown traffic.

Maggi Cole. Maggi McCree. The anticipatory smile on his lips was slightly grim as he made the association. This should be very interesting, he promised himself.

Brent looked out the car window, oblivious of anything happening on the streets they passed. For a moment, he was sequestered with painful memories he rarely allowed himself to explore anymore. "I've waited a long time for this, Maggi. A long time."

"Did you say something, sir?" the chauffeur asked, inclining his head toward Brent.

"Hmm? No, nothing, Digby. Just thinking aloud." *Thinking,* he added silently, *and planning.*

MAGGI ARRIVED A SHADE EARLY at Brent's penthouse apartment, just across the street from St. Patrick's Cathedral. She sensed that he was probably a stickler for punctuality and she meant to leave nothing to chance. To her surprise, Brent wasn't in yet, and she found herself alone with the valet.

When Brent had told her he had a valet, Maggi had envisioned someone tall, thin and stately. Wasn't there a height requirement for valets? she mused. Instead, what she saw before her could only have been de-

scribed as a cannonball with a dark beard. Saunders
was a short, squat man who appeared to have been
pumped into his uniform. When he spoke, he had a
distinctive, crisp British accent. The voice and body
didn't match.

"Miss Cole?"

"Mrs.," she corrected.

Saunders frowned slightly. It was obvious he didn't
like being corrected. He gave her a long, penetrating appraisal, then stepped aside, allowing her to
enter.

Sommerfield lived well, Maggi thought as she slowly
absorbed the surroundings. The large foyer with its
impressive chandelier provided a spacious entrance to
the apartment, a masculine atmosphere, Maggi
thought, looking toward the living room. Done almost all in white, with the floor and ceiling moldings
in a chestnut brown, it radiated a sense of openness
and yet intimacy. The setting sun permeated the room,
adding a reddish glow. She wondered if he had picked
the apartment for this effect. She would have.

"May I take your jacket, Mrs. Cole?"

Maggi jumped. She had forgotten about Saunders.
"No," she answered, "but thank you." Best to keep
the jacket on, she thought. Without it, she went from
the picture of competent feminity to an alluring female. Her dress had a plunging décolletage that dis-
played her back and shoulders to advantage. But at the
moment she wasn't sure which image suited the occa-
sion.

"As you wish," Saunders replied. "Mr. Sommerfield will be along presently." He nodded toward the living room, then carefully withdrew.

"Presently" turned out to be another half hour. Maggi tried to curb her impatience by wandering around the living room and fantasizing about the sort of man who would live here. Was he actually the conservative man Norman reported him to be, or was that just a facade? Would such a man invite a lady to dinner in his home when he could have just as easily had her removed from his office? Maggi didn't know. She hoped the ambiguity of the situation would work in her favor. She contemplated the matter as she looked out on the city, bathed in the embers of the dying sun. From where she stood, the noisy, maddening rush of people and cars was reduced to a picturesque quality.

Restless, Maggi drifted over to the huge built-in bookcase on the far left wall. It was filled with books covering all sorts of subjects. She wondered if he actually had the time to read them, or if some enterprising interior decorator had chosen them for effect. Idly she picked one up and began paging through it.

"Sorry to keep you waiting. Have you been here long?"

Startled, Maggi dropped the book. It fell with a small thud at her feet. Simultaneously, they both bent to pick it up, their outstretched fingertips brushing against one another. Maggi pulled back her hand, feeling just the faintest bit self-conscious without knowing why.

"No, not really." It was an effort not to stammer. She had wanted to be prepared for his entrance, casting a lovely image as she sat on the couch, perusing one of his books. Elizabeth Taylor in *Cleopatra*, floating down the Nile, waiting for Richard Burton to come aboard. Instead, Brent caught her being clumsy. She cleared her throat. "I've only been here for about half an hour."

"Couldn't be helped," he told her, putting the book on the shelf. His eyes never left her face. "Traffic," he said slowly, and it was clear that he wasn't thinking about traffic at all, "was horrendous. There are too many people in this city. Drink?" he asked.

Yes, she realized, she was going to need one. There was something about this man that made her nervous. Nervous in the same way that she had always been before the camera. He seemed to see too much. *Just your nerves, Maggi, just your nerves.*

"Please. Tom Collins." That should fortify her, she thought, and also give her something to do with her hands. For some reason, she was feeling slightly awkward. That hadn't happened to her before, and she had faced a legion of people in the past seven months. Stage fright, she told herself. It hit the best of them at odd times. Olivier had suffered from it at seventy. Besides, there was a lot riding on this man's approval.

Brent nodded. "Tom Collins it shall be."

Maggi followed him to the bar and slid onto one of the stools. She could see the entire room reflected in the mirror before her. The smoky glass added an ethereal look to the flagstone fireplace. Glancing over her shoulder to look at it, Maggi found herself suddenly wishing that there was a fire burning in it.

Keep your mind on the subject, she admonished herself.

She turned her attention to the "subject," who was busy mixing her drink. As Brent took out the lead glass decanter Maggi could see both sides of his profile. Absently, she wondered if he knew how handsome he was. In Hollywood, his face would have more than compensated for a lack of talent and brains and for a multitude of other shortcomings. But Brent was a high-level executive. Looks in his world probably meant nothing.

As he set the decanter back on the bar, he saw her reflection in the mirror. For a moment, their eyes held in the smoky glass. Maggi drew her breath sharply. She could almost feel his touch. *Too many romantic movies,* she thought.

"So," Brent said, turning around and handing her the tall glass, "shall we talk business now or after dinner?" He gave her what he felt was the appropriate, encouraging smile.

If we start discussing business now, he'll probably show me to the door. I'd better try to soften him up first, Maggi thought. Maybe if he got to know her a little bit, he'd be more inclined to hear her out.

She was grateful that he hadn't asked her to get to the heart of the matter, yet at the same time she was puzzled. His laid-back attitude intrigued her. She would have wanted to know what was on his mind if the tables were turned. Perhaps he already knew why she was here. Maybe he was indulging in a game of cat and mouse. There had been a number of newspaper articles detailing the projects and her involvement in it. Could he have read them and somehow remembered her name? But that had been seven months ago. She decided he was making her so nervous that she was becoming paranoid. "After dinner," she said demurely. "Although," she said, toying with her glass, "I've been told that you are all business."

He poured himself a scotch-and-soda and sat down on the stool next to her. He was too close. Maggi felt a flutter in the pit of her stomach. Perhaps the drink hadn't been such a good idea. It was doing strange things to her mind.

"Normally, I am. But I've spent a rather trying three weeks trying to charm a very *un*-charming man out of a hefty donation and, at the moment, I'm all businessed-out."

She hadn't really thought much about what an administrator of a foundation actually did. In a way, he had the same function as she did. They both made their living by trying to get people to put up money for something they themselves believed in. The similarity heartened her somewhat.

"I was looking forward to a long, hot shower and a good meal." A smile crept across his lips. "Because of you, I'm reversing the order-unless you'd care to join me for both."

Maggi nearly choked. Conservative men didn't take showers with women they knew for twenty minutes. Just why did he think she was here? She felt uneasy again. Control of the situation was slipping through her fingers. Maybe it would be best to discuss business and leave, after all.

"Mr. Sommerfield," she said formally, placing her drink on the bar, "I'm here because—"

"I invited you." He pushed the glass toward her. "Please, don't spoil it right now. I need a beautiful woman to look at and to share a few quiet moments with. Whatever your reasons for coming to see me, they'll keep for an hour—or until this headache goes away."

Again, she couldn't help wondering if he knew who she was and was just toying with her for his own amusement. "Tried aspirin?" she suggested wryly.

He waved the suggestion away, taking a long sip from his glass. The ice cubes clinked back and forth. "Never touch the stuff. Eats away at the lining of your stomach."

"How about some aspirin-free—"

He stopped her by shaking his head. Was she crazy, or was there a twinkle in his eyes? "They all have side effects."

Maggi shrugged, retreating from his pharmaceutical conversation.

He watched her as she raised her glass to her lips. "Are you aspirin-free?"

Maggi stifled another cough and put her drink down. Drinking around this man was proving to be hazardous to her health. "I beg your pardon?"

He was looking at her intently, his gaze deep and probing. Maggi felt as if her innermost secrets were being unraveled, one by one. "Do you come with any side effects? In a few hours will I regret sitting here and talking to you?" He congratulated himself that his question seemed to unnerve her. *Good. Let her be confused for a while. Let her feel nervous!*

"I hope not," she answered, mustering the most sincere smile she could project. But projecting had to do with acting, and Maggi found herself acting less and less and reacting more.

"So," he said abruptly, "what does that leave us to talk about?"

Common ground. She needed common ground. But what did she have in common with a man whose world was poles apart from hers? He might not be pleased if she brought out the similarity in their professions. Covertly, she stole another glance. What did he look like beneath that three-piece suit? Was his physique the result of good padding and expert craftsmanship? A gift from an able tailor? Or did the shoulders stay once the jacket went? And what about the rest of him? A distant urge, long banished, began to tug vaguely at the rim of her consciousness.

"Do you play tennis?" Maggi asked suddenly. The question seemed to surprise him almost as much as it did her.

"Not as often as I'd like," he confessed. "Why?"

Ah! Common ground. "Why don't we get together tomorrow at lunchtime and play a set? I'm the proud new owner of a health spa membership and it seems a shame to let it just lie there. I believe in taking full advantage of things that are offered to me."

"So do I." The words hung sensuously in the air between them.

What would it be like to kiss him? Maggi wondered, then upbraided herself sharply. From tennis to kissing—what was her mind doing? She was here to ask for money, to plead, cajole, not read for a part in *Romeo and Juliet*. Time to lighten up, she told herself. But as she opened her mouth to say something glib, she realized that Brent's focus had shifted from her face to her hair. If he were any other man, she would have guessed that he was toying with the idea of reaching out and touching it. In the right light, it looked like fiery copper. As a child, it had been her trademark. As a woman, it had been a source of attraction, drawing the eye of the beholder first to her hair and then to her.

What did he think of her? Did he find her as attractive as she found him? And what would he think once she stated her case?

"You're really very lovely." He said it as if it were a surprise to him.

He felt an attraction to her, despite everything. He reminded himself that she was, first and foremost, an actress. Actresses knew how to make themselves alluring if the role called for it. And Maggi was a handsome-looking woman to begin with. He was annoyed with himself for being affected by that, for feeling anything but the utmost contempt for her. He tried to hang on to the thoughts he had had about her earlier, that and his memories. But somehow, in the light that came from her smile, he found that it was difficult to maintain his bitterness.

He pressed his lips together and thought of Jackie.

She wished she could see into his mind. "Thank you," she murmured, casting about for something to say. Compliments made her feel uncomfortable, although she had never been at a loss for words before. But Brent and his soulful, penetrating eyes seemed to strip her mind of all thoughts.

"Dinner is served."

Saved by the cannonball in the dark uniform, she thought, almost sighing out loud with relief. Brent rose from the stool and took her hand. She liked the warm, possessive way his fingers locked over hers as he placed her hand on his arm. "Shall we?"

Maggi merely nodded as she allowed him to lead her into the dining room.

Touching her was a mistake, he thought. She felt warm and fragile, stirring feelings in him that got in the way of his motives for having her here.

How formal, Maggi thought, looking around the dining room. Another glittering chandelier sparkled at her as Brent ushered her into the chair at his right hand. She realized that she would have actually preferred sitting at the foot of the table.

Why? Why was this unsettling feeling moving through her?

As she tried to wrestle with her emotions, Brent offered her a linen napkin. Before she could take it, he was spreading it carefully on her lap. His fingers brushed against either side of her thighs. Maggi caught her breath as a throbbing sensation darted along the path he had touched.

He had heard her.

Their eyes met and held for a moment. She began to feel shaky again—just like an astronaut embarking on an untethered walk through space. What was going on here? She had been the one to talk the Ambassador Hotel into donating free rooms for all the stars who were flying out to do the show. She had been the one to wrangle that long red carpet. She had cajoled Eleanor Crosby to cut short her two-month honeymoon in order to parade across the stage in an Yves Nioche original. Why was she suddenly reduced to a nervous, uncertain woman?

"Saunders," Brent was saying, "is an excellent cook. I'm sure you'll enjoy his duck à l'orange."

Duck? Maggi felt her stomach do a flip-flop. She hated duck. When she had been on location for one of her last pictures, the director had the cast party catered and had duck flown in. The duck she'd had obviously hadn't liked the flight. It had been spoiled, and she and the duck soon parted company. She had been sick for days. Ever since then, the mere thought of consuming a duck made her shudder at the memory of the awful experience.

She realized that she must have turned pale. Brent was looking at her curiously. "What's the matter?" he asked.

Should she tell him or risk recycling her meal? He might become insulted if she refused his hospitality. It had been years since the incident, maybe she was over her reaction. "Nothing," she lied. "It's just a little warm in here."

"Well, let me take your jacket." Brent was on his feet before she could say a word. He placed both hands on her shoulders, ready to ease the jacket off. She could feel the heat of his hands through the cloth. The glowing sensation slid down her spine. Slowly she surrendered her jacket. She couldn't have played it better if she had rehearsed it.

"Lovely," she heard him say softly. The word escaped from his lips before he had a chance to stop it. He made no move to return to his seat.

"Is anything wrong?" Maggi asked, keeping her smile hidden.

"Nothing." Brent slid the navy-and-white jacket on the back of the chair and sat down. "I was just admiring the back of your dress."

Maggi smiled. *That's not all you were admiring,* she thought. "I got it in California," she told him. He looked mildly interested.

Saunders returned. In front of him he carried a silver tray on which a golden-brown duck lay on a bed of neatly arranged parsley.

Maggi fought to settle her stomach. This was ridiculous. She'd just have to exercise mind over matter, that's all.

"Oh?" Brent was asking. "Do you come from California? Or were you just there on vacation?" Did that sound too innocent? he wondered. But then, he hadn't been the actor in his family. His brother had.

If his inflection had been a tad too innocent, Maggi didn't seem to notice. "No, I live there. I'm just here temporarily."

"To plead your case with me?" he asked.

"It's a little more involved than that," she said evasively. She eyed Saunders as he began carving the duck. Her stomach churned with every pass of the knife.

"I'm from California," he couldn't resist telling her.

Maggi tore her eyes away from the offending duck. "Really?" she asked in surprise. More common ground, she thought happily.

"Yes. I lived there quite a long time ago," he said distantly.

"I miss it," she confessed, warming to her subject.

"I don't." His voice was hard. But he wiped out the effects with another smile.

So much for common ground, she thought hopelessly. Oh, well, there was still tennis.

Saunders, through with his duties, stood back, carving knife and fork in his hands like retracted swords. "Please," Brent urged, "help yourself." He indicated the dark slices that now lay next to the duck's carcass.

Maggi's tongue felt like wood. "Looks good," she mumbled, forcing the words.

"It is," Brent assured her. It was the voice of authority. "Saunders knows no equal when it comes to duck."

"What a wonderful recommendation," Maggi murmured. When she made no move to transfer the slices from the large tray to her plate, Brent did it for her. She could see by his expression that he found her behavior a little odd.

He wouldn't allow the foundation to give an odd person money, she told herself. Still, her fork didn't move to meet the fowl.

"Something *is* wrong," Brent insisted.

Did she look as green as she felt? she wondered as she shook her head to deny his statement. She knew she should say something, but the churning sensation in her stomach was beginning to cloud her thoughts.

He must think she was an idiot. With a mighty effort, Maggi sank her fork into a tiny piece of the duck. She felt a bead of perspiration break out on her forehead. Now she was sweating in front of him. Mickey Rooney and Judy Garland would have been ashamed of her. They never sweat, she thought, recalling Norman's glib comment.

Here it goes, she thought, steeling herself. One for the Gipper.

Anticipation proved far worse than reality. While Maggi knew that she would never order the meal on her own, she found that she could eat it and survive. *I have met the enemy and he is mine. The feathered enemy,* she corrected humorously, twisting the famous war adage. Now on to the unfeathered one.

She leveled her gaze at Brent.

Chapter Four

Brent studied her as he took a sip of wine. His last recollection of Maggi McCree was of her smiling broadly on a movie poster. The huge letters had proclaimed *Our Little Darling*. It was supposed to have been his brother's poster, his brother's movie. It had been entitled *Daddy's Little Man* but both the part and the title had been rewritten for the studio's newest star—Maggi McCree.

Jackie, at fourteen, had looked older than his years, much too old to play the lead in the picture. The film, Brent recalled from the stories his mother had hammered into his head over and over as he was growing up, had been especially written for Jackie. Because of one delay after another, the film had been shelved a number of times before the project finally got off the ground. When it did, Jackie no longer fit the part. But he had been counting on it. Roles for him had been diminishing steadily in the past three years and mother kept calling him a failure. Jackie had the burden of both of them on his shoulders, Brent remembered with a shudder he managed to control.

Brent realized he was staring, and he looked away.

The Maggi McCree that his mother held responsible for their plight was a far cry from the woman who was sitting across from him at the table. But it was still the same person, he reminded himself.

"More duck?" Brent urged, searching for something to say until he could clear these thoughts from his head.

No, enough bravery for one meal, Maggi thought. "No, thank you. I had a late lunch."

He accepted her explanation and Maggi took care not to sigh with relief. All in all, she thought she had given more to the actors' cause in the past half hour than she had in all the previous seven months.

"My compliments to the chef," she added. *Don't overdo it, they might give you a doggie bag.*

Saunders emerged at that moment from the kitchen, carrying before him an assortment of French pastries on a silver serving tray. The rich, fancy confections were in direct contrast to the man's somber deportment. His expression looked decidedly sour as he regarded Maggi's plate. A slice of the offensive fowl was still left.

"It was very good," Maggi said as he cleared her plate away. "Really." *With a reading like that you would have flunked your audition Maggi my girl.* She certainly didn't seem to convince Saunders.

"Thank you, madam," he said icily. Saunders left the tray on a side table at Brent's elbow.

"Where did you find him?" Maggi asked, watching the door close behind the valet's formidable body. Except for the beard, he made her think of Peter Lorre. All he needed was an evil laugh.

"Saunders?" Brent glanced over his shoulders. "He's been with me for years."

How unfortunate for you Maggi thought, but forced a smile on her face. Why would anyone want someone so dour haunting his living quarters?

"Do you turn a different shade when someone offers you French pastries?" He was smiling broadly.

He had noticed her reaction to the duck, she thought, momentarily embarrassed. Well, no better weapon than the truth. "French pastries never made me ill." She made a selection from the tray, a tall, rich chocolate affair with swirls of whipped cream adorning the top.

"And duck has?" Brent asked, surprised. "Why didn't you say something?"

"I didn't want to insult your hospitality. I didn't think that my complexion would give me away."

He touched her cheek and gently slid his fingers along the beguiling hollow he found there. He stopped, hesitating, struggling with his own conflicting feelings.

She shivered as a warm sensation flowed from her cheek and eventually encompassed all of her, its intensity remaining intact as it spread. The shiver had been an involuntary reaction, only a tiny external movement. She hoped he hadn't noticed.

"I'm afraid it did," he told her. "You must need to speak to me very badly."

The liquid green eyes looked up at him, making him forget himself for a moment. *God, she is beautiful! Jackie would have been handsome, if he had been allowed to grow up.*

It was time to stop setting the scene and go through with the reading, Maggi thought. "Yes, I do."

He dropped his hand to his side, suddenly realizing that he was still touching her face. "Fine, after the brandy."

"Brandy?" she asked, her fork suspended over her dessert. Why did he keep erecting detours in her way? Now that she had started, she wanted to get to the point, to get her little speech over with. She had never felt this nervous during her entire acting career, and the nervousness hung over her head like a heavy sword.

Brent leaned forward and gently covered her hand, pushing the fork down toward the tempting fare. "After dessert," he clarified, "I have an excellent brandy I'd like you to try."

He was issuing her a temporary stay, she thought. Why? Was he trying to set up a romantic evening between them? It would've been a nice thing to believe, but there was something in the air, something that was making her feel more uncomfortable than the situation warranted. Something wasn't right here. But what?

What wasn't right, she told herself, was the way she was reacting to Brent. She was disturbed because she felt so unsettled around him. Part of her wanted to get this over with while another part hoped the evening would last as long as possible. Neither part wanted it to end abruptly, and it might, it very well might, if she pleaded her cause straight out. Seduce the man's senses, was that it? Well, she thought as she slowly raised the last piece of pastry to her lips, the man was seducing hers, no doubt about it.

She caught herself. She was trying to be sexy. *Better stop this. When he finally finds out why you're here, he might misconstrue all this.*

Brent rose, took her arm and led her to the living room. He needed to move, to clear his head.

This time there was a fire crackling in the fireplace. Two goblets framed a bottle of brandy, all neatly arranged on a silver tray by the fire. If she were going to write a romantic scene, this would have been the setting she'd use. Anticipation began to prick at her.

Damn it, Maggi, remember why you're here.

Brent lifted a goblet in one hand and the bottle in the other. "Try this and tell me how you like it." But just as he began to pour, he stopped. "Unless, of course, brandy makes you ill."

"No, no bad effects from brandy," she assured him.

"That's good to hear." He began to pour again. "Wouldn't want to waste this. Sampling brandy can be a sensuous experience."

He *was* out to seduce her, she thought in surprise. He certainly was different from the man she had met in the office, or, rather, the man she had been prepared to meet. That would explain why he had been studying her so hard at the table. He was probably planning his mode of attack.

The Seducer Gets Seduced. Not bad for a title of another bedroom farce. Except they weren't making those anymore. They were making teenage sex romps. Maggi smiled. It was a million-dollar smile, according to Norman. She wished it was worth a quarter of that. More than that, she wished she didn't have to ask for that sum, or any other. She would have liked to enjoy this evening and let things happen as they might. For the first time since she couldn't remember when, she felt physically attracted to a man, enough to know that the strange, high-strung feeling in the pit of her stomach was not due to unsettling memories of a duck on location, or the effects of an excellent brandy. The effects belonged to Brent Sommerfield.

"I really shouldn't be taking up your time like this," Maggi began, feeling that it was definitely time to put her cards on the table. If she didn't talk now, she might not have the courage to, or the desire. The room, the brandy and, most especially, the man were making it harder and harder to keep her mind focused.

"As I recall," Brent said, slipping an arm about her shoulders, "you weren't holding a gun to my head when I tendered my invitation to you."

"No, but..." *C'mon, Maggi, where's your glib tongue?* Lost, she thought lightly, lost somewhere in the first sip of brandy.

"Come here," Brent said, taking a step toward the large picture window. He kept his arm about her shoulders so she had little choice but to follow—even if she hadn't wanted to, which she did. "Look down there." He pointed with the goblet toward the street far below. "I bought this place for the view. Up here it's rather serene and peaceful. Even the constant rush of the city takes on a tranquil beauty. All those busy, scurrying people mix into a benign whole, don't you think?" he asked, looking back at her.

What I think is that if you don't kiss me, I'm going to kiss you. The thought was so strong that for a second, Maggi was afraid that she had said it out loud. But Brent's expression hadn't changed, she noted with relief. The words only echoed in her head.

He hadn't wanted to play it quite this far, but something urged him on, something kept him from allowing her to state her business. If she did, he would calmly have to turn her down. That was what this evening was all about, initially. Her defeat and humiliation. He had wanted the satisfaction of turning her down. It wasn't much, but it would have paid her back a little for Jackie.

If you lead her on, it'll be that much more poignant.

But was he leading her on? Or was he simply stalling because of something else? Was he deliberately trying to prolong this because of some other motive? He wasn't sure and it bothered him. Uncertainty was foreign to him. He had built up his life being very, very sure of all his motives.

It was hard to shake something that had been instilled in you almost since the very beginning. He re-

membered his mother's voice. It was raining and
hardly anyone had come to the funeral. "It's all Maggi
McCree's fault." She had tried to breed hate into him,
but she hadn't totally succeeded because he had broken away. With a great deal of work and not a little
luck, he had managed to make some very fortunate
real estate investments that now provided him with his
present life-style. His work at the foundation was a
way of sharing his luck with the less fortunate. He had
sent his mother money dutifully even in the beginning, when there had been none to spare. Conscience
money. Had his sudden plan when he saw Maggi in his
office this afternoon sprung out of a feeling of conscience as well? Was he only going through the motions here?

No, he owed it to Jackie. Jackie had been . . .

The first rays of moonlight caught in Maggi's hair
and blended with the light from the fireplace. Flam-
ing copper, not at all becoming to a singing, dancing
moppet but very becoming to the woman standing
within reach.

Brent's arm tightened about her shoulders as he
bent his head and kissed her.

This wasn't part of the plan.

Work it in, a voice inside his head urged before he
stopped thinking.

His kiss was just what she had imagined it to be—
warm, sensuous, overwhelming. Reaction wound
through her veins at lightning speed, not like the
brandy that had trickled through slowly. Maggi
could have sworn she heard the music from the film

From Here to Eternity. At least in her head. It was from the beach scene, just as the waves come up over Burt Lancaster and Deborah Kerr.

Fade out. Mayday. You're here to plead a case, not seduce a man or be seduced. What's he going to think if you let this go too far? That you're trading yourself for a few dollars? Okay, okay, a quarter of a million. A high price, but a price nonetheless. You have to level with him. Now.

Later, another voice responded, pleading for just a moment more. An exquisite, wonderful moment more.

It was amazing, she thought later, that they went on kissing with their glasses still in their hands and not a drop was spilled. And not a sensuous moment was sacrificed.

His lips moved over hers gently, as if he were restraining himself. Yes, maybe this was the reserved man Norman told her about, but reserved men don't start to kiss women they hardly know.

What was she doing, writing a guidebook for the corporate executive?

Maggi stopped thinking altogether and let herself drift for a luscious eternity. Brent's free hand pressed her closer to him, lightly stroking her back. The pressure of his lips deepened, then lightened, as if he was at war with himself. She made it easier for him. She kissed him back with an intensity that had long been missing from her life. It was as if a spontaneous combustion had gone off in the room. Her reaction to

Brent was instantaneous and complete. Maggi felt almost drunk from the impact.

She wasn't quite sure, when it was over, who had stopped first, he or she. Everything was a momentary blur.

She carefully drew a deep breath, hoping it would steady her racing pulse. Norman had warned her about this. He had said she was set to explode one day. Norman knew about things like this, she mused, still slightly dazed.

"I'm afraid the evening isn't going quite the way I intended." She wanted somehow to let him know that she hadn't planned on using her body to gain her way.

He took her lead, relieved that he didn't have to mask his own bewilderment over what had happened. "Oh?" he asked, nodding toward the sofa. She took his cue well. *An actress. Remember at all times, she is an actress.* "And how did you want the evening to go?" He kept the conversation light, as if to deny the unexpected effect she had had on him.

If you tell him, that might be the end of what could be a beautiful interlude. Hell, she wasn't here for a beautiful interlude, she argued. She was here because of the benefit. She owed something to the people she had garnered together for the show.

And what do you owe yourself?

Honesty, she answered.

"All I wanted to do was get you in a mellow mood to listen to me." Her voice had never sounded shakier.

Brent spread his hands wide. "I'm as mellow as I'll ever be," he assured her.

Plunge in, Maggi. "I represent an organization that is putting on a benefit show in order to renovate the retired actors' home and their hospital." He crossed his arms before him, looking a little too innocent, she thought, but that could have been her own guilt coming to the fore. She should have told him this *before* the kiss. Only there might not have been a kiss if she had.

She hesitated.

"Yes?" he urged her on.

This was going very badly. She had never had any trouble talking about the benefit before. But then, neither had she kissed anyone she was pitching to before. If she kissed, it was at the end of the deal, a simple, grateful peck on the cheek. There had been nothing simple about the kiss that had passed between them.

"Well, to be quite blunt, I'm in a bind. We've run short of funds. I need your money."

"My money?"

You sound like an adolescent, selling your first box of Girl Scout cookies. Where's your showmanship? Your savvy? They would have taken away Mickey and Judy's tap shoes for this pitiful display. "I mean the foundation's money. The Wallaby Medical Research Foundation." Maggi cleared her throat. "Let me start over again."

"Please do." He should be enjoying her discomfort. After all, this was what he'd had in mind all along, wasn't it? To make her squirm, to make her uncomfortable. So why did it feel so empty?

The velvet feel of her lips still lingered on his.

To his surprise, Maggi put out her hand. "Hello, my name is Maggi Cole and I was wondering if I could have a little of your time."

She did it so guilelessly that he had to laugh. "I don't think you have to go quite that far back to start over."

"I'm beginning to think I do, in order not to give you the wrong impression."

He sat forward, placing his hand on her bare shoulder. The skin beneath his palm felt smooth, tempting. He was reacting again. Was she acting this way on purpose? He knew his mother, had she been watching, would have immediately said yes, but he wasn't his mother and her venom had not become his own, no matter how hard she had tried.

Jackie's sad eyes came back to him, haunting him.

"And what impression is that?" Brent asked, hiding his thoughts.

"I don't usually approach business from this end."

"What end do you approach it from?" The question was meant to lead her.

"From the hip, with a little violin music if possible." Maggi smiled a bit contritely. "Seriously, it really is a very good cause. These people have brought entertainment and joy to millions of people in their time, and now I don't think they should be forgotten and cast off just because they're no longer attractive or capable." His penetrating blue eyes were making her feel almost tongue-tied. "Brent, I don't know why I'm stating this all so badly. Norman always laughs about my silver tongue."

"Norman?" Her husband? It hadn't occurred to him that she was married. Until seven months ago, the Maggi McCree he'd had in his mind was an eight-year-old. He had never thought of her as growing up, getting married, having a family. Jackie had never had the chance.

"Norman Everett. The producer. He half raised me. He's responsible for the second half of my life—or so he'll tell you when he gets the chance." She paused. "Will he get the chance?"

"What?" She caught him unawares. He didn't understand what she was driving at.

They'll never give you the silver tongue award again if you keep this up, she thought wryly. "I know that what I've just blurted out here isn't going to convince you to let me speak to the board about lending their support to our cause. I thought perhaps you'd like to meet with Norman—"

"No," he answered. Here it was, his final salvo.

If he had meant to sink her, he had misfired. Maggi did not sink easily. "Okay, no Norman. But I would like a chance to introduce you to some of the people involved in this project before you give me your final decision."

"Maggi—" he began, thinking that the charade had gone on far enough.

She anticipated his words and put her hand up, stopping them. "Please. I know I haven't gone about this very well."

Does she know how appealing she looks, pleading? Of course she does, that's why she's doing it. He tried to separate himself from the slow, seductive feeling winding through him, but his eyes remained trained on her face. The soft glow of the light from the fireplace kissed her cheek, making him long to do the same.

"Let me have another chance, a longer chance, to make you see that there are few better causes to support."

"What is it exactly you're asking for?"

She thought it best not to discuss the sum just yet. "Your time, for now." Time; it was growing short, she thought, but this couldn't be hurried. She had to make him see how important this all was. "I'd like to take you to the theater," she said suddenly.

"What?"

"To a show," she added enthusiastically. "Do you go to Broadway shows, Brent?"

"No. I haven't the time."

It was true. The pace of his life kept him busy enough. On the few outings he allowed himself, there had been visits to the opera and the ballet, more at his date's insistence than of his own desire. He purposely ignored the Broadway theater. And he never went to the movies, had no interest in the world of glitter. It had all killed Jackie, and out of respect Brent had denied the movie world's existence. He didn't let it touch his own—until this moment.

She knew it took all kinds to make a world, but she couldn't fathom ignoring the exciting world of the theater, especially since it was practically at one's fingertips.

"Then you should make time," she said easily. "You have no idea what you're missing." *God, he's going to be a hard nut to crack. Norman was right about him. But not about the other point. No, a warm, vibrant man lives within that stuffed shirt.* One kiss was all that it had taken her to realize that. Maggi felt heartened.

"I have a feeling you're going to try to show me," he said dryly.

Maggi nodded, her smile dazzling. "With all my might." She rose. "Well, I've monopolized you long enough," she announced. "I'll be in touch, Brent." *Now to go home and plan this out carefully so you don't make a mess of it just as you nearly did here.*

"Wait," he called as she began to pick up her jacket. "I'll drop you off." Brent surprised himself.

Maggi turned. "I can get a cab," she told him without too much conviction.

"It's dark outside," he pointed out.

"So it is," she answered, looking not at the window but into the deep blue abyss of his eyes. What secrets lurked there? she wondered.

"Lovely women should not be out alone at night."

"I never argue with a possible angel," she answered, letting him take the jacket from her hands.

He stopped helping her on with her jacket. *Her flattery is getting a bit thick,* he thought. "I'm hardly an angel," he muttered.

Maggi laughed at his obvious misunderstanding. "No, not the kind with wings. The kind, if you'll forgive me, with money. Angels," she repeated, "financial backers of shows. You really don't know much about the entertainment world, do you?"

He shook his head.

"Well, Mr. Sommerfield, your education is about to begin."

"We'll see, Maggi, we'll see."

Chapter Five

"And then what did he do?" Norman asked. He had cornered Maggi the first chance he had the next morning. Actually, it was closer to noon when he had finally made it in. He had taken one of the assistants out the night before to show her the New York City that he remembered. The New York City he remembered had become more exhausting than it used to be.

But he forgot about how tired he was in the light of this new development. He narrowed his brows into a dark shaggy line and waited for Maggi to continue.

"And then he brought me home," she said, finishing her narrative. Or so she thought.

"And?"

"And I shut the door."

He leveled his gaze at her suspiciously. "What side was he standing on when you shut it?"

Maggie laughed, setting aside a stack of messages she had to return. "Honestly, Norman, you sound like my mother. No, I take that back. My mother never asked questions like that."

He wagged a reprimanding finger at her. "That's because when she was asking the questions, you looked like an undernourished chicken." Maggie opened her mouth to protest his rather uncharitable description. "Oh, yes, I remember. I was there. You were just skin and bones. No—" he searched for the proper word "—meat." He cast a discerning eye at her figure. "You've filled out some since then."

Maggie began patiently. "Except for that one lone kiss, Brent Sommerfield was a perfect gentleman the entire evening." Too much so, maybe. *Now, Maggi, don't let your imagination run away with you. You hardly know the man well enough to play Scarlett to his Rhett.*

Norman appeared unconvinced. He scratched his head, ruffling the fringe of hair.

Maggi stood up and brushed it down lightly. "Not every man behaves like you on a date. And don't give me that big, innocent look," she warned with a warm smile. "I've heard about you."

"All lies," he protested, waving away both her statement and her hand from his head.

"A man like you should have better things to do than chase girls who are young enough to be his daughters."

"A man like me *needs* to chase girls who are young enough to be my daughters. It keeps me young." He bristled. "I thought we were talking about you."

"No, we were talking about Brent Sommerfield. Why are you so down on him, anyway? He may prove to be the solution to all our problems."

"I just don't want you to become the sacrificial lamb."

The phone rang and Maggi scowled at it accusingly, waiting for Ethel to answer it. It took Ethel five rings. She was going to have to speak to her, Maggi thought wearily. Now what had they been discussing? Her attention span seemed so short lately. There were just too many things to remember.

"Norman, I'm not a wide-eyed teenager fresh off the bus from Hot Coffee, South Dakota, so—."

"Hot Coffee isn't in South Dakota," he corrected, "it's in—"

"Well," she cut in, slightly irritated, "wherever it is, I'm not from there. I'm Hollywood-born-and-raised, and I know every trick in the book used to bed a lady, so stop worrying." She stopped shuffling papers, the search for her elusive address book temporarily abandoned, and looked at him for a moment. "Norman, we had this conversation yesterday. What's eating you?"

Norman shrugged. The motion caused his entire marshmallow-soft body to ripple. "Just a hunch, that's all. There's something familiar about him."

"I thought you said you'd never met him."

"I haven't. It's his name that bothers me."

His answer struck her as being rather odd. "That's ridiculous. You can't carry a grudge against a man because of his name."

"I," he said, drawing himself up to his full five-foot-four stature, "am Norman Everett. I can do whatever I want." Then his voice became more serious. "I worry about you, Maggi."

"For heaven's sake, why?" He sounded more like the father figure she had come to cherish than her mentor and business associate. She had to admit she loved him for it.

"You've been driving yourself too hard."

"I'll be fine," she assured him. "The show's two and a half weeks away. I promise, after we come up in the black, I'll go on a long vacation. If we come up in the red—" she sighed "—you'll find me doing dishes in the cafeteria at the local Y."

But he wasn't listening to her glib humor. "Don't do anything foolish, okay?"

"Like go over the falls in a barrel?"

"Like fall in love."

She rolled her eyes. Norman had a fierce imagination when he so chose. "Norman, the man just kissed me. You kiss me all the time."

He leaned over her desk, his tie fluttering into a stack of telephone messages. It sent them sliding down into the other stacks of papers. He wasn't concerned with her papers; he was concerned with the look he had seen on her face when she talked about Sommerfield. A look, he ventured a guess, that she wasn't even aware of. But he had seen it before on other faces, too many times. And Brent Sommerfield, from what he had heard, was a cold, exceedingly efficient business executive. He didn't want to see Maggi hurt. "You never talked about any of those times breathlessly."

She refused even to acknowledge what Norman said. "Here, look this over," she said, sticking a script into his hands.

He lifted it. "This must have taken five trees to produce. What is it?"

"The final form of the script for the show. I want your opinion."

He dropped it on her desk with a thud. "It needs to lose ten pounds," he commented flippantly.

This time, she placed it into his hands forcefully. "Read it."

"I don't have to read it. I know. Maggi, how many times have I told you? Never—"

"...put on a show longer than the audience's seat can comfortably tolerate," Maggi ended. "I know, I know. But just read this, okay?"

"For you," he said, kissing the top of her forehead, "anything."

"See that you remember that."

Maggi smiled as she watched him close the door. Norman was a darling, but he had no reason to worry about her getting involved with Brent Sommerfield. She wasn't sure exactly what had come over her last night, but she felt certain that in the light of day, away from glowing fireplaces, warming brandies and threatening ducks, she would be fine. Maybe it was just her own loneliness coming to the fore. There was no denying it; there were times when she was lonely, very lonely. Her feelings were no reflection on her daughters. They were the light of her life and she loved them dearly, but her love for them didn't fill up all the spaces she had inside. There was still an emptiness, a loneliness within her. It was a different kind of loneliness. She was lonely for the kind of companionship a wife counted on from her husband. That certainly didn't fit Brent Sommerfield in any manner, shape or form.

Her smile broadened as she thought of the man. The way to get to him was to blitz him. Not let him have a moment to dwell on whatever reasons he had for disliking the entertainment world as much as he did. Put in the proper frame of mind, people tended to be more generous. She intended on putting him there. After all, it wasn't as if she were asking him for a quarter of a million of his own money. And it was for a worthy cause. All she had to do was convince him that it was worthy.

Maggi went through the blue avalanche that Norman's tie had created. Each note represented a message that either her secretary or she had taken. She had seen enough blue notes in the past seven months to redo her entire hotel suite twice over.

The top one caught her attention. She buzzed Norman.

"What? I haven't finished reading yet," he complained into the mouthpiece.

"Do me a favor, Norman," she asked prettily, slipping into a Southern accent.

He could just picture her batting her eyelashes at him for effect. "Don't I always?"

"Edgar Blankenship is coming in on TWA Flight Number Six at one today. Meet him for me?"

Norman sighed. "I don't know if there'll be enough room in the cab for me and His Highness's ego." He pushed his glasses on top of his head. "Not that I blame you for not wanting to meet him, but what are you going to be doing?"

"Scoring, I hope."

Norman's black coffee came dangerously close to striking up an acquaintance with the script Maggi had given him. His last swallow rebelled and fought its way up to his throat. "What?" he sputtered between coughs.

"Tennis, Norman, tennis. I'm only going to be playing tennis."

He had never known her to take a break once she got involved with a project. He was the one always telling her to ease up. This didn't sound like his Maggi. "Are you going to tell me what's up, or do I have to come marching back into your office and beat it out of you?"

"You're playing Mother again."

"I almost choked to death on this coffee; you owe me an explanation."

"That's because you had Ethel make coffee you can eat with a fork," she reminded him.

"Never mind how I like my coffee. Who are you going out to play—Sommerfield?" he guessed suddenly.

"You always were sharp. I'll fight to the death any man who says otherwise."

"They wouldn't dare," he answered drolly. "And don't try using your silver tongue on me."

"My tongue was pure lead last night," she remembered ruefully.

"If it was, how come he's taking you out to play tennis?"

"*He* isn't," Maggie corrected. A smile of determination filtered across her face as the plan formed in her mind. "I'm taking him."

INSTEAD OF A TENNIS OUTFIT and a light-blue-and-white sweater, she should have worn a heavy overcoat, Maggi thought. Even that wouldn't have cut the chill in the look that Brent's secretary gave her. The guard at the gate had been too stunned by her appearance to give her any argument about her right to see Brent Sommerfield. Only lunatics and luncheon dates came waltzing up, brandishing a tennis racket and wearing an outfit that did spirited things to a man's imagination.

Marietta, of course, was another story. "And what is it you want this time?" she asked coldly. "Did you make another appointment with another fictitious secretary?"

"No." Maggi smiled easily. "I have a date with Mr. Sommerfield."

Angrily, Marietta glanced at her appointment schedule. "You're not on here."

Maggi leaned lightly on her tennis racket, her coppery hair dipping against her cheeks. "It's not that kind of a date. If you'll just let me into his office—"

"I think not."

"Marietta, dear," Maggi said in her sweetest voice, sugar with an iron underlining, "Mr. Sommerfield is not going to be pleased with your behavior."

"Then he'll tell me," Marietta retorted, crossing her arms before her.

"I'm sure he will. In no uncertain terms."

Marietta glanced at the closed door down the hall. It was true that he hadn't said anything to her about this—this woman returning today, especially not dressed to make a spectacle of herself. But she had overheard him inviting her to his apartment. Perhaps the witch was telling the truth—probably for the first time in her life.

Marietta pressed her thin lips together, making them disappear entirely. "All right," she picked up the phone, "I'll ring—"

It was all the headway Maggi needed. "Don't bother. I'll announce myself."

"But you can't *do* that," Marietta cried as Maggi passed her. Maggi was at Sommerfield's office, opening the door within seconds.

"Oh, but I just did."

Maggi eased herself in quickly, closing the door behind her.

That was how Brent first saw her that day, her hair slightly disheveled, tumbling over her shoulder, wearing a brief tennis skirt that highlighted the longest, most enticing pair of legs he had ever seen.

His hand was on the phone. He had been about to make a call, but he forgot it, forgot everything but the captivating woman who had just darted into his office. For the second time in two days.

"Someone after you?" he asked.

"Your secretary," she answered as the door moved behind her. "With a hatchet, I think."

Marietta shoved her aside as she pushed open the door. She grasped at the doorknob to steady herself. "Mr. Sommerfield, I tried to stop her—"

"Whatever for?"

Marietta was crestfallen. "Then you were expecting her?" She felt cheated. She had been looking forward to having the woman unceremoniously ousted from the office.

"It would appear so. I'll ring you if I need you."

Marietta left, defeated. Perhaps she could get a transfer, she thought. She had been with Sommerfield for five years now and she had liked his business-only attitude. There had been no wife and mistress to juggle the way there had been with two of her last three bosses. No girlfriends calling at all inconvenient hours. Just business and more business. It had been his most appealing feature. It now appeared to be a thing of the past, she thought dismally.

A recording that suggested he try to dial again reminded Brent that he was still holding the telephone receiver. He replaced it, then slowly walked around to Maggi.

There was no doubt about it, the woman was beautiful from all angles. He idly wondered how her acting career was going. From what little had seeped into his consciousness, films were far freer than they had

been back in Jackie's day. He wondered how many
nude scenes she had done. And how many men had
possessed her, mentally or physically? No, wait, hadn't
the article he read stated that she was a producer now?
The recollection brought an unconscious smile to his
lips.

She liked his smile, Maggi thought, gaining courage from it.

"Is this one of the outfits in the show?"

"Hardly," she said, laughing. "We'd have to glue
the audience into their seats if it were."

"Afraid they'd leap on the stage?"

"Afraid they'd leap for the exits." She didn't realize that he was paying her a compliment. "Nearly half
the tickets are going to members of the industry.
They're expecting a high, high fashion show. Things
to make their eyes pop out."

"So far, I see no contradiction," he answered softly.
His eyes moved over her slowly before he raised them
to her face.

Maggi felt her heart hammering faster and faster.
*Save your energy for the game. At this rate, you'll pass
out after the first serve.*

"Maggi," he said, placing his forefinger beneath
her chin and raising her head, "I do believe you're
blushing." *How had she managed that?* he wondered.

"I'm not used to compliments."

He looked surprised. "I thought people in your
world were into compliments quite heavily."

She detected a disparaging note in his voice, but thought better of becoming defensive. After all, what he said was true. She just didn't like the way he said it. "It's a way of life," she agreed. "But genuine compliments are another story."

He wondered how much she knew about the word "genuine." "If you're not modeling something from the show for me, why are you—?"

"Tennis," she said, executing a quick swing to emphasize her point. "You said you played."

"Yes, I did." He still didn't see— "Fine, let's go." She linked her arm with his, urging him toward the door.

"Go?"

"To play tennis."

"But it's Tuesday."

She stopped. "Is it against your religion to play tennis on Tuesdays?"

He laughed despite himself. "No, but—"

She looked up at him and gave him her best smile, "Then what's the problem?"

"Maggi, I don't know how it goes in your world, but I can't go running off in the middle of the day to play tennis."

"Got a meeting?"

"No."

"Luncheon date?" she asked, peering into his face like a persistent child.

"I'm having some sent in."

"Deadline to meet?"

"I always have deadlines to meet."

"How soon?" she pressed, refusing to be defeated. "Maggi—"

"Did you know that playing tennis is good for people our age? Gets your blood moving again." She twirled the racket between her hands. "I suppose it's because you have bad legs, huh? Don't like to be seen in shorts?"

"Yes, I know about tennis being healthful and my legs, for your information, are in fine condition." He knew she was baiting him, but he couldn't resist answering.

Maggi eyed his trouser legs as if cutting them away with her vision. She looked back at his face, a grin marking hers. "Prove it."

"Maggie, this is insane," he protested, but he was already letting her lead him out the door.

"Life is insane," she countered. "It's up to us to find whatever moments we can and make sense out of it the best we know how."

Marietta's head snapped up at the sound of Maggi's voice. She took one look at the situation and jumped to her feet, her hand hovering over the phone. "Are you in need of assistance, Mr. Sommerfield?"

"I don't think so," he answered, laughing, as the elevator door closed on them.

Marietta shook her head and took out a copy of her résumé from its place in back of the top drawer. It was time to update it again.

"AND JUST WHAT do you propose I play in?" Brent asked after Maggi gave his astounded driver the address of the health club she had joined yesterday.

Maggi settled back in the seat. "I'm sure they can outfit you there," she told him, pleased with herself. *Step one. Unstuff the stuffed shirt on a regular basis. Show him that life is fun.*

"You look like the cat that just swallowed the canary," he commented.

"Just anticipating a good game."

"Tell me, just how does all this fit in with your plan to—"

"Shh." She put a finger to his lips. "We're not supposed to talk business, yours or mine. This is purely for fun."

He doubted it. He knew that, at bottom, there was a motive behind everything she did. But at the same time he found himself being swept away by a hurricane named Maggi. Once again, he began to think that perhaps the animosity he had carried with him always in the back of his mind was unjust.

"Since we're going to be playing together," Maggi said glibly, "is there anything you want to know about the woman who's enticed you into showing off your legs?"

Brent caught the curious look that Digby gave him in the rearview mirror before he fixed his eyes back on the bumper-to-bumper midafternoon traffic.

"Nothing much comes to mind," he said. *I know all I need to know about you.*

"You're an unusual man, Brent Sommerfield. Well, for the record, I'm a producer. It's my job to part people from their money and make them like it." She waited to see him smile, but caught instead another deep, probing look. Did he resent the flippant way she described her work? Did he think she was drawing a comparison to his career? *Weigh your words carefully with him, Maggi.* "Or something like that," she amended. "Are you sure there's nothing on your mind?" she prodded. "Other than all that work you so justly left behind you?"

"Nothing," he assured her.

He really was unusual, she thought. Most people she met outside of show business usually had all sorts of questions beginning with, "Is it true that—?" But then, Brent shunned show business, didn't he? Maybe he really didn't have any questions. A rare man.

She glanced at his rugged, strong profile. A rare, handsome man, she thought, feeling just a tingle of anticipation again.

BRENT WAS OUTFITTED with no trouble at all. The health club was more than happy to show him what the well-dressed tennis player was wearing these days. Within ten minutes after their arrival, Brent was wearing a light-blue-and-white pullover with an animal insignia and light blue shorts that showed Maggi that his assessment of his legs was not based on blind vanity.

"Hmm," Maggi said as they walked down the corridor toward the tennis courts, "you were right."

There was a crowd of people in front of them. "About what?"

"Your legs. They're not ugly." She looked down at the muscular definition. "As a matter of fact, they're quite well toned. Closet athlete?" she guessed.

"I bicycle on Sundays when I get the chance."

The light entered her eyes. "How fortunate."

He caught the pregnant tone in her voice. "Don't tell me you're going to whip out a bicycle next."

"No, not now. But I'm free on Sunday." It was a lie; she was never free anymore. But if she stayed up late Friday and Saturday night, she would be able to clear Sunday.

She certainly wasn't shy, he thought. But then, she had a goal, a motive, he reminded himself.

And so did he.

Chapter Six

Brent watched as Maggi stopped, turned and waved before she disappeared into the side entrance of the MacKenzie Theater. The sparkle in her eyes made her look like a young girl. The thought took Brent back to his own youth.

"Back to the office, sir?" Digby asked with uncertainty after a moment of silence had passed.

"Yes," Brent answered quietly, lost in thought.

Why did she have to be so damned attractive? Rejecting her bid to speak to the board would be far easier if he had never met her, if she had just approached him via a telephone call. Seeing her, being with her, was taking the edge off his desire for revenge. As a matter of fact, he was beginning to feel somewhat uncomfortable with what he planned to do, what he *had* to do. And Brent Sommerfield didn't like being uncomfortable. His attraction to Maggi made him feel disloyal to the memory of his brother.

Brent shut his eyes and thought back to his childhood, to a time when he had been very, very young.

He could remember a tremendous house filled with people. Now he knew that they had been servants; then he had just thought of all of them as people who fawned over his brother. Jackie was the center of everything then. His mother's pride. Jackie had been discovered at the age of four, and for seven years he was the reigning child star on the lot. Everyone loved Jackie.

Brent was no exception. He had felt awe and love for his brother, and envy unmarred by jealousy. Brent had always been shunted to the side by his mother, treated as nothing more than an afterthought. He could remember wishing for a father so that each of them could have a parent to love him, but he never knew who his father was. All he had been told by his mother was that the somber-faced man in the one worn picture he possessed had never amounted to anything. He wasn't allowed to dwell on the subject. There had been parties and laughter, and he had hung on the sidelines, absorbing it all.

Then, slowly, the parties stopped, then the laughter. Brent remembered standing in the middle of the huge house, stripped of its rich furnishings, with his suitcase at his side. They had to move into something they could afford, a smaller house. Temporarily, his mother had said.

The places became progressively smaller, more sparsely furnished, yet crammed. Crammed with recriminations and quarrels. His mother, Brent later learned, had gone through a good deal of Jackie's money, mismanaging it for him, sinking it into bad investments, spending it lavishly to ward away insecurity. The courts had long ago instituted the Coogan Act in order to prevent parental drain of a child star's earnings, but there were ways around it for people who were clever. And his mother was clever.

She was also sharp-tongued. Jackie was no longer her darling. He became, in her eyes, just like his father, a quitter, a failure. Things continued to go badly, a toboggan ride down the slope of anonymity.

But even during that time, there were good moments. He remembered the long talks he had with Jackie. He could remember little of the conversations, just the feelings they shared. But while Jackie always treated Brent with far more affection than their mother did, he had grown into a spiteful person. Jackie had literally transformed before Brent's eyes. He had become bitter, bitter with the star system that caused him to be usurped by a younger, brighter star— by Maggi McCree.

Maggi became their scapegoat. If it hadn't been for Maggi, things would have been different. Brent heard the refrain every day; it became a steady diet. The criticism became more vicious as their situation worsened.

Then came the blackest morning of Brent's life, the morning he found Jackie's lifeless body in the kitchen, an empty bottle of sleeping pills and a half-consumed pint of whiskey lying next to him on the table. At seventeen, his adored brother was a has-been, washed up, used up. No one wanted him, no one but Brent. In his young mind, Brent had blamed Maggi. It was all Jackie had talked about in the last days of his life. If it hadn't been for Maggi, he would have had that last part rewritten for him, would have impressed the powers-that-be with his growing skills. But no one wanted to listen to a maturing child star as long as there was a younger, cuter child to take his place. That younger, cuter child had been Maggi.

Brent stared out the window, unseeing.

"SO HOW IS CHRIS EVERT LLOYD doing this afternoon?" Norman asked several hours later. He walked in to find Maggi, as always, hip deep in paper.

Maggi glanced up and smiled, looking, Norman thought, radiant. How did she manage it? he wondered. "He beat me," she announced.

"Good for him. I sure would like to beat you myself for forcing me to spend the last two hours with the almighty Blankenship."

"Blankenship's a good choreographer, Norman," she reminded him.

"Blankenship's also a royal pain. Do you know that we had to switch his room? It made him feel—" Norman put his hand to his forehead dramatically, "—too crammed. It cut off his creativity. Nine hundred square feet and it's squeezing him," he said in disgust. He brushed off a chair and sat down. "Why does this business attract so many prima donnas?"

Maggi pushed aside the list of changes she was incorporating in the taping schedule. "Because the public has a love affair with them. You can't imagine what it's like, Norman, to have people try to reach out and touch you wherever you go, making you feel as if you're special, as if your mere existence is a gift to them." She realized that she was letting herself get carried away for a moment, then stopped. "Heady stuff, adulation."

The brief moment had been enough. "You do miss it, don't you?" he pressed.

Maggie shrugged. There was no point in denying it. "Sometimes, when I feel tired, unappreciated, when I can't get the normal, everyday things done. Being prince or princess of the world is a terrific feeling. You begin to expect it, need it." The nostalgic smile passed from her lips, to be replaced by a wry one. "Sometimes, it's surprising when you find a levelheaded person in this mad world of ours."

"You turned out damn well."

"I had a mother who constantly reminded me that this, too, would pass." Maggi smiled ruefully. "Too bad she couldn't have carried her common sense over to her business deals. Any con artist with a glib tongue made a target out of her. Oh, well." She sighed. "What's past is past."

"I wish Blankenship was past. He has no right to act as if he's a star. He's a choreographer. A damn paunchy one at that."

Maggi looked at Norman's own growing girth but kept her smile to herself. "But he's been fawned on. He can make an absolute klutz look as if he were born dancing. That's his gift. His payment is revered homage."

"And a hell of an asking price," Norman added. He recalled Blankenship's fee for the one special he had produced.

Maggie raised her finger to make a point. "Which he is waiving, don't forget."

Norman rose slowly. His body ached. "How can I forget? He reminded me seven times in the space of two hours. Well, I'm calling it a day."

"Hot date?" Maggi mused.

"Hot tub," he corrected. "I've got to admit it," he groaned, "this old body's not holding up the way it used to. I've got aches in places I never knew I had when I was a young man."

"You'll never get old, Norman. You'll go on forever. It's in your contract." Maggi winked, looking back at her schedule again.

"Why don't you go home?" Norman suggested.

"In a little while," she promised vaguely. "I've got some catching up to do."

"Can't it keep until after dinner?"

The voice making the suggestion did not belong to Norman. Maggi's head jerked up. Brent was standing in the doorway. After a beat, she realized that Norman was still there, guardedly eyeing Brent the way a knight might regard a visiting emissary of unknown allegiance who was coming to call on his queen.

"Brent." His name was framed in surprise. Once again, she was struck by his appearance. The man got better looking each time. She wasn't going to be able to stand more than a few visits, she thought wryly.

Your mind is beginning to fail. First signs of battle fatigue. "I thought of sending out—"

"Bad thought," Brent said, walking in.

"Norman Everett, Brent Sommerfield." Maggi introduced the two men as she rose to her feet. She saw them eye each other the way fighters do before the first round. Brent put out his hand first.

Norman took it, offering what Maggi could tell was a forced smile. "Yes, we tried to meet."

"I beg your pardon?" Brent looked at him strangely. His general feelings had been correct. Everyone connected with show business was a little crazy.

Down, Norman, Maggi thought. *This is no time to act protective.*

"I was the guy you wouldn't see," Norman clarified, still smiling his broad smile.

If he meant to make Brent uncomfortable, he failed. Brent was used to holding his own quite well. "Marietta takes her job rather to heart. She feels it's her duty to protect me from everyone but the heads of teaching hospitals and colleges."

"Marietta?" Norman asked, looking not at Brent but at Maggi for an explanation.

"His secretary."

"Ah, the bulldog." Norman recalled her description.

Maggi felt as if she wanted to crawl away.

Brent grinned broadly, knowing that Norman had to be quoting Maggi. "That's rather an apt description," Brent agreed genially.

"Don't you have a hot tub to see to?" Maggi asked Norman before he could say anything else that might get her into trouble.

Norman hesitated, then relented. She was a big girl now. That was the problem, he told himself. He had to stop taking this paternal attitude toward her. Still, he promised himself to have this fourteen-karat-gold executive checked out. There was something about the man that was nagging Norman.

"Yeah, I do, at that. Nice meeting you, Sommerfield—finally," he couldn't resist adding. "And you, get in early," he warned Maggi.

Maggi saluted. "Yes, boss."

"Is he?" Brent asked once Norman was gone.

"Is he what?"

"Your boss?"

"No, not anymore. It's rather a partnership now, although he keeps telling me I'm in charge. He's a wonderful man," she said, feeling the need to keep talking. She didn't know why, but suddenly, she felt very nervous being alone with Brent in such a small space. He seemed to fill up every nook and cranny.

"Um, Brent, I don't mean to be rude, but what are you doing here?" she asked as she watched him look around her office slowly, taking in the clutter, the stacks of papers.

Damned if I know. And he didn't. Half an hour ago, he had planned to go home and review the crucial points of the McCaffery report before tomorrow's meeting. And there was that research grant to that enthusiastic young internist he had promised to take under advisement. He certainly didn't lack for work, even after hours. But somehow, he found himself walking down to his limousine and giving Digby the address to the MacKenzie Theater. He felt himself being drawn to her like iron filings to a magnet. She had not left his mind since this afternoon.

"I decided to take a chance that you were free for dinner. Are you?"

She looked back at the programming schedule she knew should be completed tonight. "Well..." she began hesitantly.

He took her arm. "Fine. Where would you like to go?" he asked.

She didn't bother to mask the look of surprise that came over her. It seemed as if they had reversed roles since this afternoon.

As if he read her mind, he said, "Turnabout is fair play. You whisked me away from my work. Now I'm taking you away from yours."

"Take me, take me," she pretended to plead, sighing wearily. "I wonder if any of those people who watch television have the faintest idea of all the effort that goes into putting on a show." She gestured at the piles of paper everywhere.

"They wouldn't be interested," he assured her. "Most people only care about the end product."

He had that right, she thought. She reached for her coat, but he was there ahead of her. "What is Saunders whipping up tonight?" she asked uneasily, remembering last night. Saunders, she decided, was the type of man who probably reveled in revenge. How many ways were there to prepare duck?

"Saunders has the night off," Brent told her, ushering her to the door.

"Then where—"

"We're eating out," he answered briskly, walking toward the elevator.

Maggi took his hand and led him to the stairwell.

"It's quicker. The elevator takes forever, even though there are only three floors."

The stairwell was poorly lit, and just for the moment she felt as if she were threading her way down into the bowels of a secret cavern with her own special prince in tow. *That's what comes of growing up in a fairy-tale world,* she thought. *Your imagination runs riot first chance it gets.*

Logic notwithstanding, a happy glow began to fill every space in her body. There was no doubt about it; she liked being with this man, even if there hadn't been a project and money to see to.

"I thought you hated restaurants," she said when they reached the ground floor.

He held the door for her, then followed her out. "I'm discovering things about myself I never knew," he answered.

In a manner of speaking, it was true. Since Maggi had burst into his life yesterday, he had begun to re-evaluate things about himself, about his past. He found himself taking out old thoughts he had held as gospel and examining them again.

"If you can force yourself to eat duck on my account, I can try a restaurant on yours," he told her matter-of-factly. "Which suits you?"

"I'm fond of Top of the Six's."

"Top of the Six's it is. Digby?"

The chauffeur nodded his head. "Yes, sir."

And they were off. Off for a sumptuous dinner. Maggie tried not to think about the work she had left behind. It was much more fun thinking of Brent.

IT WAS EASY not thinking of work when she was with Brent. What was difficult not to think of was how attracted she was to him. Coming from the glamorous world that she did, Maggi was leery of any relationship based on physical attraction. A lot of the men she encountered were merely eight-by-ten glossies—lots of shine, little depth. But there was something about Brent, something in his eyes more than anything, that captivated her. She saw an entire battery of emotions there—pain, sorrow, wariness. And they were all, she thought, somehow directed at her. Yet his mouth was quick to smile and his gestures were all so courtly toward her.

He was a puzzle, a damn good-looking puzzle. And she was in the mood for solving one.

"Tell me," she said as they lingered over their after-dinner cordials, "what is it that you have against the entertainment world?" She knew it was a loaded question, one that might very well throw the fat into the fire. But she thought if she approached him honestly, if she asked him straight out, maybe he would tell her. Then she would know what she was up against and could begin to untangle the knot.

He was silent for a long, long moment. Part of him wanted to tell her, tell her everything. About Jackie, about his mother, about the hatred that had existed in his life, hatred aimed at her. What would she say if she knew that there were people who actively held her responsible for their fate? It would surprise her, that much he knew. Would she care? Or would she toss it off with a shrug of her shoulders, a toss of her coppery hair?

No, he didn't think so. Knowing her for only a short time, he somehow felt that she wouldn't be so blasé about it, but he couldn't be sure. Maybe he was giving her absolution where none was deserved. He owed her nothing. He owed Jackie a lot.

He couldn't tell her. It would be sharing too much. Despite feelings to the contrary, there was still a part of him that couldn't let go of the past. It could still all be an act on her part. Actresses were supposed to be able to fool a camera, gull an audience into believing they were Joan of Arc, or a downtrodden flower girl with a cockney accent, or any one of a hundred characters. Perhaps she was playing a part right now, a part she was playing in order to win what she wanted.

Brent looked at his drink, staring at the dark liquid that coated the sides of his delicate glass. "First, I find it offensive that people are paid such high sums of money merely to make a movie."

"Do you hate sports?" she countered quietly.

Where did that come from? "No, but—"

"Athletes are paid astronomical sums. Granted that both fields are overpaid, but that's the public's fault, not the athletes' or the actors'. It's only human nature to grab as much as you can when you can. There's no telling what tomorrow has in store for you." She grinned. "Next reason?"

"Next, I think you should stop probing, don't you?"

Maggi fell silent for a beat. "I just want to know what I'm up against," she said quietly.

He regretted his words the moment he said them. "You make it sound like a war."

"Well," she said philosophically, meeting his gaze head-on, "you haven't told me that I can get an appointment to present my case to the committee of advisers. That is what they're called, isn't it?"

At least she's honest. "Yes, that's what they're called. All in due time, Maggi. All in due time. You still haven't convinced me that the cause is worthy. I owe the committee the benefit of my judgment. If I allowed everyone who approached me with his hand out to speak to the committee—"

"—They'd never get to go home to change their clothes. I understand."

And, in an odd way, she did. She had a lot of respect for someone who believed in doing his job to the best of his ability. But her ability was going to outdo his. She had to break down his resistance.

She looked as if she believed the evening was over, he thought. It *was* getting rather late. They had lingered here longer than he had expected, yet he didn't want her to go.

"I still have that brandy," he began, his eyes inviting her.

"Are you asking me to your place for a nightcap?" she asked.

"Yes."

What else are you asking me there for? No, she couldn't let anything else happen, she thought. As attracted as she was to him, as much as she felt that there was a layer of this man that needed touching, needed understanding, she couldn't let anything happen between them until she knew where she stood. At bottom, business couldn't interfere with pleasure, and vice versa.

Maggi found herself riding the elevator up to his penthouse.

"Just one quick drink," she said, looking at her watch. "I have an early appointment tomorrow."

"So do I," he told her. The elevator stopped at his floor.

"And I'm a positive bear if I don't get enough sleep." She was rattling on. Maggi forced herself to hold her tongue.

"I have the same problem."

Was he making fun of her, or letting her know that he saw through her?

The apartment was deserted-looking. Maggie recalled that the ever-efficient Saunders was out for the evening. That meant they were alone—all alone, looking down on a darkened world beneath their feet with a shower of stars winking overhead.

Maggi backed away from the window. She was going to have to get a rein on 'her thoughts or she would wind up seducing herself for him before he ever laid a hand on her. She backed up against Brent and his chest felt hard against her back.

Slowly, he turned her around until she faced him. More slowly, he lowered his mouth to hers, sampling her lips the same way he had sampled the brandy last night. First a little, then a little more, until all his senses were engulfed with her.

Maggi felt a heady, overwhelming sensation travel through her veins. She was breathless within moments. He pressed her body against his and she felt an urgency igniting. His mouth trailed along the outline of her chin. He buried his face in the silken mass of her hair. His breath feathered out along her neck, making her burn with anticipation at the very same time that she was telling herself to hold back.

"Maggi," he whispered into her hair.

"Yes?" she asked, her voice husky with the battle that was going on within her.

"Stay with me tonight."

Chapter Seven

For a moment Maggi thought she had imagined his words, conjured them up through her own growing desire. But it was Brent's voice she had heard. The words were real, and so was the dilemma. She wanted him too much to say yes.

For the first time she damned the cause into which she had poured all her energies for over half a year. Although it had brought her to him, it now stood in the way like a sharp-eyed duenna watching her charge. If she stayed, if she gave in to the fire in her blood, then she would run the risk of having him think it was only because of the benefit. It would make for all sorts of problems down the road. Relationships could be difficult at best. Starting one under the present conditions would be problematic. He might think that she was bartering her body for the money her organization needed so badly. He wouldn't understand that she didn't sell herself at any price and that she had felt something intense and powerful respond within her the very first time she had seen him, the first time she had heard his voice.

What had come over her? She hardly knew this man. And yet, she felt she did know him, as the soulmate she had lacked for so long. Or at least, she wanted to believe that. Maybe Norman was right. She *had* been alone too long. A product of the world of make-believe, maybe Maggi was afraid of what reality might be like.

There were so many reasons to say no. And only one reason to say yes. The word trembled on her lips, seeking escape. She pressed them together, taking a deep breath to still her pulse. It went on beating erratically.

"I can't," she answered quietly.

He had cupped her face in his hands, his fingers delving in her hair. He had hands, she thought the first time she had seen them, like a fine pianist—long, delicate, yet strong. She felt that strength now as his hands tightened just a little before they slipped away from her face.

"Why?" There was no pleading intonation in his voice. It sounded as if he were asking to have something explained at a committee meeting. His eyes did not betray the fire in his blood.

Damn principles, damn complications, damn everything, she thought in frustration. Maggi turned away and looked out the window. She wished she were down there, amid those people, hurrying off somewhere. This was harder to do than juggling temperamental high-strung actresses.

"Because I don't know you," she said, seizing the first thing that ran through her mind. "Because you might misunderstand. Because I don't sleep in strange beds." The last excuse was made in hopes of keeping the situation light, but it was the truth. She didn't sleep in strange beds or, rather, with strange men. She had been—Norman had laughed at her time and again—as chaste as a nun. That was what made this so much more difficult.

The nun wants to recant her vows.

She turned to look at Brent, hoping that he understood what she was telling him, understood without taking offense.

If he takes offense, he just wants a warm body next to him and it wouldn't matter whose. If that's the way he is, you don't want him.

Oh, but I do.

He kept silent for a long moment, looking at her until Maggi felt positively stripped of all her thoughts, all her outer trappings. "You think I'm trying to take advantage of the situation, don't you?"

Diplomacy, coupled with honesty: that had always been her chief ally. "I don't know you well enough to make that judgment. And you," she hastened to add, "don't know me well enough to determine whether or not I might be taking advantage of you. So," she said briskly, pushing the tense moment away, "shall we have the brandy and call it a lovely evening?"

"We'll have the brandy," he agreed, beginning to pour, "but I'm not sure about calling this a lovely

evening." He presented her with her glass. "We seem
to be at a curious Mexican standoff."

"Mexicans, I hear tell, are a very warm and friendly
people." She smiled over the rim of her glass, her eyes
twinkling mischievously. "Whatever is meant to be,
will be." *Please let it be meant to be. Get hold of
yourself, Maggi,* she told herself sternly. *The next
thing you'll do is a poor imitation of Doris Day singing* "Que sera, sera."

He had never asked a woman to spend the night before. He had never had to. Things like that always
progressed naturally, informally. To ask and be re-
jected was a doubly unfamiliar experience. Heaven
help him, she both intrigued and stirred him. He
found himself wishing that Maggi McCree had grown
up to become an avaricious, selfish bitch who bore the
mark of years of indulgent living. Maggi Cole looked
as if she had a portrait in the attic wearing her few
sparse venial transgressions while she went on appearing far younger than her years.

He wished fervently that Maggi and her gala benefit had never come to New York.

And yet, he was glad she had.

MAGGI COULDN'T PUT her finger on it, but something
was bothering her. She had this nagging feeling that
there was something more between her and Brent than
just the sticky problem of money. It was there, she realized the next day as she sat at her desk, taking a
momentary break, in the way he looked at her when
he thought she didn't see. At times, she could have

sworn she saw an accusation lurking within the shadows. But why?

"You're just overworked. Norman said that it would catch up to you sooner or later," she muttered out loud as she locked her fingers together over her head and stretched back.

She needed that spa desperately today, she thought. But there was no time. There were a thousand details to see to. Although she knew that part of being a success at anything was the ability to delegate responsibilities, there was absolutely no one outside of Norman whom she had faith in to carry out all the minutiae that were involved in the show. The list of things was endless. When she did allow someone to take care of something for her, she found herself double-checking the work just to be sure that it went right.

This whole benefit might be a group effort, but it was her name on the bottom line. If this failed, people wouldn't remember that a thousand and one people were involved, they would just call it Maggi Cole's white elephant.

Maggi wasn't partial to white elephants.

But she was, she thought, wrapping a strand of hair about her finger, partial to Brent. Once all this was over, she'd let him see just *how* partial. If he was still interested. She had to keep him interested until then.

"Interested in the show. Get him interested in the show, Maggi," she reprimanded herself. Her first loyalty had to be there. Her heart was there, not to mention her reputation. The entertainment community had a horrid tendency to remember the failures in glaring red lights. The successes faded like June roses in the fall.

She did have an excuse to see him, Maggi told herself, her mind drifting back to Brent. After all, she had promised to indoctrinate him. She had a feeling that until and unless she did, he was not about to broach the subject of the benefit to the board, let alone allow her to give a presentation to them.

If only she could understand why he looked at her the way he did sometimes.

Ethel, her temporary secretary, walked in, humming "Some Enchanted Evening" quite loudly. Also, quite off key. Maggi could see why Ethel belonged to a temporary employment agency. A few weeks of the woman was probably all anyone could stand. If inefficiency had a name, it would have been Ethel Shulman. But Roxanne, Maggi's own personal secretary, had suddenly had to return to California ten days ago—something to do with her grandmother's failing health.

Maggi scribbled a note to herself to remember to send flowers. She hoped it wouldn't get lost in the many other notes she had been scribbling all day. The pile was multiplying faster than two love-struck rabbits during mating season.

Ethel had been hired to tide things over until either Roxanne came back or the show was over. Maggi had thought she could make do with any secretary until then, but she was wrong. Ethel wasn't a secretary, she was a perpetual auditioner. She wanted to break into show business in the worst way.

Yup, that about described it, Maggi thought, listening to the woman hum—the very worst way. She doubted that in all her years in show business she had heard a person with less talent.

Maggi ignored Ethel's nasal finale. "Are the letters ready to sign yet?" she asked.

"Which letters?" Ethel blinked, disappointed that Maggi said nothing to her about her rendition.

In the woman's defense, Maggi had to admit that things were getting terribly hectic around here, but she had a feeling that Ethel wouldn't have been able to keep up even if things were peaceful.

"The ones I gave you yesterday morning. To the creditors," she further elaborated.

"Oh." The light slowly dawned in the woman's myopic eyes.

Maggi stood up and put her hand on the short, amply proportioned woman's shoulder. "Ethel, if this is all too much for you, just say so. I'm sure that Powell, Inc., can send over—"

"Oh, no!" The look on Ethel's face was pure horror. "Please, Ms. Cole. This is the closest I've ever gotten to show business. I'll get right on those letters," she cried, dropping a shower of blue notes on Maggi's desk. "I promise."

Maggi sighed. Oh, well, it was only another two weeks. She'd let her stick it out until then. Maybe, Maggi thought hopefully, sitting down again, Roxanne's grandmother would take a turn for the better. She made a note to stop at St. Patrick's and light a candle to St. Jude, the Saint of Impossible Causes.

Danny Thomas had sworn that the reason he was a success today was because of the bargain he had struck with the saint in his heart all those many years ago when he was a starving, struggling performer. If it could work for Danny Thomas, maybe it could work for her. Who knew, maybe St. Jude was soft on show people. It was worth a try.

She certainly could use a little celestial help right about now. She— Maggi's thought stopped as she looked down at one of the notes that Ethel had deposited on her desk. It was from Brent. Maggi lost no time in dialing. Maybe he had called about the foundation.

Maybe he had called about her.

Whatever the reason, her pulse was doing double time by the time she finished dialing.

"Mr. Sommerfield's office."

There was no mistaking the crisp, frosty tones. Maggi wondered if Marietta could be persuaded to give efficiency lessons. On second thought, she preferred Ethel's plodding good intentions to Marietta's icy competence.

"Is he in, please?"

"Who shall I say is calling?"

Hold onto your bustle, sweetie. "Maggi Cole."

"I'm afraid—" Rejection ran clearly in her voice.

"I'm returning his call," Maggi said, breaking into Marietta's excuse.

A large sigh preceded her statement. "I'll see if he's in."

Maggi could just see the pinched lips disappearing as she growled out the words. A sharp click told her that Marietta had stabbed the hold button.

Peaceful music filled the air. *He can't hate entertainment that much. At least he's not having the stock market report piped in.*

Maggi began to hum quietly to herself. The music was from one of her favorite shows, *Brigadoon.* Without realizing it, she began to sing softly. "Come to me, bend to me, make me your own..."

"What?"

Maggi sat up, brought to attention by the confused male voice on the other end. "Sorry, I got carried away with your Muzak," she apologized. "This is Maggi Cole."

"I know," he answered easily.

She was pleased that he recognized her voice, but he added, "No one else I know would sing to me."

"Everyone should be sung to at one time or another," she said humorously. "Remind me the next time we're together."

"Which is why I phoned."

"Yes?" Did that sound too eager? After she had turned down his invitation to stay the night, she worried about what the rejection might have done to his male ego. On the spur of the moment, as he was bringing her home, she had told him she had theater tickets for tonight. She had sent Norman out first thing this morning to cajole front row tickets from the Albania's manager.

"I'm afraid I have to cancel tonight. I seem to be coming down with something." Damn, he wasn't any good at lying. But he didn't want to see her again, couldn't see her again. He had given it a lot of thought after he returned home last night. He was giving up on prolonging any sort of revenge. He wanted her out of his life. Feeling strong emotions for her wasn't right; they just didn't reconcile themselves with what he felt over the loss of his brother. He wanted to erase the whole situation, pretend it never happened. Thank God she had had the presence of mind to turn him down in this one moment of weakness.

Think fast, Maggi. "Cold feet," Maggi said brightly.

"I beg your pardon?"

"What you're coming down with, Brent Sommerfield, is a case of cold feet. You're afraid that you'll like what you see tonight."

I already like what I see. That's the problem. I like it far too much for my own good. Turn her down, now. Make the break clean and final.

He couldn't.

"I had no idea you held a degree in medicine, Dr. Cole," he said mockingly.

"Absolutely. Did my residency in Hollywood. I know all about cold feet. And nervous stomachs. I'll be at your office in two hours. Be sure to put a muzzle on Marietta."

She hung up before he had a chance to decline.

She stared at the phone for a moment. Well, she had certainly brazened that out, she thought with a smile.

The phone began to ring again. She rose, watching it warily as if it were a cobra ready to strike at any moment. If that was Brent, she wasn't going to give him a chance to talk his way out of going tonight.

"Ethel," she called out, walking quickly by the tiny cubbyhole where Ethel sat at her desk. "Get that for me, will you?"

"Where will I say you'll be?" the woman asked uncertainly.

"Out, lighting a candle. Maybe two."

She checked her purse for quarters just as she came to the stairwell. She was going to need an army of candles before this thing was over.

LEAVING ST. PATRICK'S more amply lit than usual, Maggi made her way back to her office feeling a little better. She took the side entrance, but rather than going back to her office, she stopped by the theater for a moment to see how things were going onstage.

An array of young, eager girls, wearing a rainbow assortment of leotards, tights and leg warmers, were all gathered about Edgar Blankenship, hanging on his every word as if he were delivering the Sermon on the Mount.

As it should be; Maggi was certain that was what Blankenship thought.

"Any creativity on this stage will be mine, do I make myself clear? I am not looking for another Ann Miller or Gwen Verdon. I am looking for an equivalent to the Rockettes."

You're looking for blind obedience, Maggi filled in mentally.

She scanned the hopeful faces. There were, at a quick perusal, over fifty dancers. Twenty were needed for the show.

Maggi walked away, not wanting to see who was going to be cut. She never did have a heart for that part of the business. She was glad that casting was not her department.

But in a way, she realized, it was. She had had to turn away offers from people volunteering to do the show. The flood of telegrams increased as the deadline drew near. Would-be greats who were only mediocre in their field were now supplicating her. They wanted to share the stage with the incredible gathering of stars she had assembled. There wasn't room for everyone. Her list had been complete for over a week.

"No" was the cruelest word in the English language, she thought as she made her way up the stairs. She wondered if she would be hearing it from Brent tonight.

Not, she decided with a determined set of her jaw, if she could help it. She decided that she needed to relax just a little before she went to meet him. Maggi dashed up the stairs to her office and placed a call to her daughters. Talking to them always made her feel better about everything.

"WHAT IF I HAD HAD something contagious?" Brent asked when she walked into his office.

It had taken him a moment to phrase the question. She was wearing a kelly-green dress that was temptingly slashed up the side of her right leg while the rest of it romanced her body.

"It would be a small price to pay if I can get you to see things clearly," she said cheerfully, pleased with the admiring way he looked at her. Underdogs, one; nonbelievers, zero.

"Your way," he guessed.

She gave him the sweetest smile he had ever seen, a smile belonging to an innocent. *She is quite an accomplished actress,* he thought.

"But of course," she answered. Just then, his phone rang. "It's six-thirty," Maggi protested as he began to reach for it.

His hand hovered over the receiver, then withdrew. "So it is, and I promised you dinner, didn't I?"

"Dinner." She nodded. "And I provide the show." The look he gave her said that he wished she would. Maggi felt another deep blush rising from her chest until it colored her décolletage with a rosy hue that was not unbecoming to her kelly-green sheath.

The phone stopped ringing abruptly. "See, they'll call back in the morning," Maggi assured him, taking Brent's arm. "By the way, what did you do with Marietta?"

"I couldn't find a muzzle, so I sent her home."

They walked to the bank of express elevators. "Does she usually stay this late?"

"Always. She's very dedicated."

"She's very something, all right," Maggi agreed, watching the door of the elevator open. A man and a woman were inside, locked in a warm embrace. They apparently hadn't expected anyone to be getting on at that time of the evening and they sprang apart self-consciously. Maggi stole a covert glance at Brent to see what his reaction was to the romantic twosome. Nothing but amused tolerance. She had her work cut out for her. Didn't believe in show business. Didn't believe in love. The man was a challenge, all right.

"AREN'T YOU EVEN CURIOUS as to what show we're going to see?" she asked as Digby drove them to the theater. She settled back in the limousine and studied him, waiting for his answer.

The broad shoulders shrugged beneath the blue-gray jacket. "One's pretty much the same as another, I'd imagine."

"That's where you're wrong," Maggi said, leaning forward. She noticed with warm satisfaction that as she argued Brent's eyes had a tendency to slip from her face down to the soft cleavage her dress exposed. The look in his eyes was flattering. "If you could imagine, you'd know that there's a world of difference. There are comedies, musicals, mysteries, dramas, things to make you think—"

"Of what a colossal waste of money and energy it is to have grown people playing dress-up and make-believe," he ended.

"Life's awfully hard, Brent," Maggie said seriously. "Sometimes we need these magicians to create a different world for us, to make us forget our own troubles and relax, feel a part of something else, share a joke. I suppose you don't read, either," she said mischievously.

"Of course I read."

"Something other than the newspaper?"

To humor her, he ticked off a list of things that he had read, books that she had noted in his apartment on her first visit.

"Well, what do you think Jonathan Swift's *Gulliver's Travels* was?" she asked, referring to the last book he had mentioned.

"Satire," he answered without hesitation.

"Make-believe," she countered. "It was satire at bottom, but it was dressed up. Otherwise, the bitter criticism wouldn't have been palatable. Even churches had their morality plays to get messages across. Surely you're not going to be more reserved than the medieval church, are you?"

The look on her face was serious. But it was the kind of seriousness affected by an imp who would burst out laughing merrily at any moment. Puck in *A Midsummer Night's Dream*. She didn't look a thing like Puck, he thought, but she was pure magic nonetheless.

"All right." He laughed. "You win—for now."

"One inch at a time, that's all I'm asking," she said happily as they approached the restaurant.

No, he thought, you're asking for a lot more than that and I don't know if I can give it to you.

Chapter Eight

Laughter, Maggi felt, was a wonderful gift from the gods, and she knew she needed all the help she could get. So she decided to take Brent to a Neil Simon comedy, a wonderful, entertaining comedy filled with one-liners and just enough seriousness to give the theater-goers pause at the end of the play. The audience left the theater feeling good about itself.

When pressed, Brent grudgingly agreed that he had enjoyed himself. Especially after Maggi repeated the lines that had made him laugh, mimicking the different characters' voices. She seemed, he thought to himself, armed to the teeth to try to win him over.

His impression was reaffirmed the following night. This time, she was dressed casually. She wore a simple, ice-blue wraparound dress. Nonetheless, she was stunning. She would have looked stunning, he decided, wearing aluminum foil. He was so busy observing her that it took several minutes before he realized that she was carrying a picnic basket.

"And just where do you propose to have a picnic in this part of town?" he asked as they walked out of the elevator and onto the street. Aside from the incongruity of it all, the sky was cloudy overhead and rain threatened to make its appearance at any moment.

She patted the wicker basket, which she had stumbled upon in the wardrobe department that morning. "In the movies," she answered cheerfully.

"Maggi, I'll be the first to admit that you're a constant source of surprises, but—"

"It's not really a picnic," she hastened to add before he could turn her down. "Just a couple of sandwiches. You do like pastrami, don't you? Everyone likes pastrami."

He smiled over her assumption. He detested pastrami. But then, she had endured duck for him. No, not for him, he corrected, for that damned benefit of hers. "Just as everyone likes the movies, right?"

She grinned. "Now you're getting the hang of it."

Gracefully, Maggi slid into the limousine ahead of him. He watched her hips as they swayed slightly before she sat down. Brent became aware of an increasingly hungry feeling haunting him. He wanted her, wanted her in the worst possible way. A sexual appetite had never played a dominant role in his life. Even when he was an adolescent and his high school locker room was thick with stories of who did what with whom, Brent was always too interested in getting ahead, too interested in making something of himself, in shedding the devastation of poverty that clawed at his throat like a hungry tiger, to take note.

Later, as his business acumen stunned men who had far more experience than he did and his fortune began to grow, he found that he did not care to compete in the sexual arena, playing the games that men and women played. It was as if his sexual drive had been channeled to one purpose, conquering his oppressor: poverty. Not that, when the opportunity arose, he turned his back on sexual companionship. It just wasn't something he went out of his way for.

But he sought it out now; he sought *her* out now. He had promised himself as he dropped her off last night that there would be no further meetings between them. It was wrong and no good could come from it. Even if she wasn't who she was, she was still part of the industry, the industry that had ground Jackie to dust.

Yet, here he was, sitting next to her in the limousine, going to see his first movie in twenty-eight years.

There was only one answer for it. *The woman's a witch.*

"Where to, sir?" Digby asked, his massive hands poised about the steering wheel.

"I haven't the faintest idea," Brent answered. "Probably to Oz."

His answer left Digby utterly confused, but it brought a broad smile from Maggi. "You *do* know the name of a movie," she marveled.

"Oz was a place in Frank Baum's book," Brent pointed out, refusing to admit anything.

Nonetheless, Maggi felt as if she had scored a point for her side. "Radio City Music Hall, Digby."

"You're taking a picnic basket to Radio City?" Brent asked incredulously.

"If it embarrasses you, I can put the sandwiches in my purse," she offered with a wink.

"If you want to look like little Red Riding Hood, I don't mind. But didn't Radio City close down?" He vaguely remembered reading that the theater had been steadily losing money and had closed its doors some years back.

"They still open for special occasions. Right now, they're having a film festival. A revival."

He frowned, wondering what she had in store for him. "I'm afraid to ask what they're reviving."

"Musicals."

He did not bother to disguise his groan. "I'm afraid you just hit the limit."

"Brent..." Maggi began.

He raised his hands to stem the flow of protesting words. "The idea of people breaking into song at the drop of a cue is more than I can stomach."

"All right, so maybe people don't break into song at the drop of a hat—"

"Maybe?" he echoed in disbelief.

"...but the least you can do is listen to the words. A lot of those songs *say* something."

"Yes, that the song writers are happy that most of the public is dumb enough to be taken in by all this nonsense."

What made him so bitter? she wondered. What secret lurked in his past to have soured him so badly? "If it was all nonsense," she said patiently, "Bob Hope wouldn't have trekked to all corners of the world for years, bringing his Christmas shows to all those soldiers.''

''That was a humanitarian act,'' he answered. ''That was different.''

''Was it?''

''Yes. If you're in some godforsaken corner of the world through no fault of your own, you'd probably listen to a chimpanzee crooning 'Dixie' if it made you think of home,'' he insisted.

Maggi shook her head. ''It's not different. It's all one and the same. It's entertainment. Its function is to lift souls, to join kindred spirits, to bring across messages that would otherwise not be understood—like *Gulliver's Travels*.'' Her eyes never left his. There was a definite challenge in them.

''You don't give up, do you?''

''Nope.''

Brent took out a white handkerchief and waved it. ''Are you sure you're not a lawyer?''

Maggi pointed to the handkerchief. ''Does that mean you'll go?''

''I suppose it can't hurt.''

''Absolutely painless,'' she promised.

He doubted it. There was pain in going into the huge theater with its majestic lobby. There were vague memories tied in to all of this. He had often tagged along to the various studio sets to watch as Jackie went through his paces. One of his first recollections of Jackie was seeing him on a soundstage, playing a young prince in a musical version of *Arabian Nights*.

Maggi appeared to be in rapt attention. He watched her face in the light that streamed from the screen. She was mouthing the words to the songs, totally oblivious of the fact that he was watching her and not the screen. He set his mouth grimly. She was part and parcel of the industry. There was no divorcing them.

"C'MON, ADMIT IT," Maggi urged when they came out four hours later. "You had a good time."

"If I had a good time, it was the company, not the circumstances."

"If?"

"You're being coy," he said.

Maggi batted her lashes twice. "Whatever it takes," she told him, unabashed. "I haven't got much time to convince you that entertainment is a wonderful thing." She looked at the chauffeur who was slumbering peacefully, slumped in the front seat. "I think we're out past his bedtime."

"He's not used to my keeping late hours."

That made Brent's accompanying her that much more of an accomplishment, Maggi thought triumphantly.

"I'll arrange for a matinee next time," she promised.

He was about to wake Digby. Instead, he turned to face her. "Maggi, I don't think there should be a next time."

"Of course there should," Maggi insisted. Her cheerfulness masked her mounting panic. "Brent, I know that I must seem like a pushy female to you, but this really *is* an important cause. Do you know that one of those people we saw tonight died in obscurity, totally penniless, totally alone? No one there to care for his last needs. People flock to Hollywood every day to grab a bit of the stardust. They don't know about the brutality of the business.''

The look that Brent gave her frightened her so that she took a step back. There was almost a savageness about it.

''It's the worst business in the world. Why put up a hypocritical front?'' he asked.

The man who occupied the newsstand on the corner ceased gathering his papers as he stopped to listen to these two people arguing next to him. Maggi became conscious of his staring at them. She turned to glare at him, but he went right on staring.

''I'm with him,'' he said, jerking a newspaper-printed thumb at Brent. Maggi ignored the grubby man.

''What hypocritical front?'' she asked Brent, her voice growing tight.

''Putting on the benefit. Pretending that all those glittering people give a damn. Why go through all this to rebuild a hospital and a retirement home when the industry spews out corpses like some heartless god expecting sacrifices every hour?''

Something was terribly wrong here. There was a personal reason why Brent was so opposed to what she was doing. Why wouldn't he tell her?

Rather than withdraw, Maggi put her hand over his. She gave it a gentle squeeze. She wanted to encourage him to talk. The more he talked, the more likely it would be that they might get to the heart of the problem. But he fell silent, embarrassed by the outburst that had been triggered by memories he could no longer keep locked away.

"It's not hypocrisy, Brent. It's to make up for some of that. To make up for the pain of rejection, be it the studio's or the public's. The public's very cruel, you know. It can love you, worship you and toss you away the next day when someone new comes along."

"Yes, I know."

His answer baffled her. She waited for him to continue.

He didn't.

"Well—" she cleared her throat "—I'm sorry if tonight upset you."

Now what? Do you frantically look for another foundation? Do you offer the creditors your third-born?

"Forgive me," Brent said. "I've been under a strain lately."

The newsstand man sighed. The excitement was over. Too bad.

Brent's hand curled around her wrist, reminding her how susceptible she was to his mere touch. "Let me take you home."

She nodded, wondering if she was being a fool to go on hoping that she could break him down. But she had to keep trying, she told herself. For a lot of reasons.

BRENT'S OUTBURST had bothered her all night. It still hung over her like a black cloud the next day. If she couldn't convince him, she couldn't get an appointment with the board. It was as simple as that.

Yet the matter wasn't simple. His reaction to the situation bothered her because it was the reaction of a man with a painful secret. The look in his eyes had belonged to a vulnerable man who was trying to cope with—what?

She couldn't sleep.

Finally, she managed to drop off at dawn, forty-five minutes before her alarm clock performed on cue. In order to have time to try to convert Brent, Maggi had had to reshuffle her work. That meant early mornings, very early mornings. She wondered if anyone besides security men and pigeons was up.

Somehow, she made it through her shower and down to the office, although she couldn't quite recall any of the motions in between. The fog stayed with her through the first few hours. Haunted by Brent's words, she found that she wasn't getting anything accomplished.

What was the reason for that terrible look in his eyes?

"MAGGI, WE HAVE TO TALK."

Maggi looked up as Norman walked in. She had been struggling with a budget that refused to be trimmed in any manner, shape or form. She was relieved to find an excuse to take a break.

"I feel as if I'm trying to carve a Thanksgiving turkey that's been hand carried from the Bowery. There's nothing left to—What's the matter?" She stopped in midsentence. Norman looked as if he were going to tell her that someone died.

"We're not going to get the money from the Wallaby Foundation."

Had he heard something she hadn't? "What makes you say that?"

"I just found out who Brent Sommerfield is."

What is he driving at? Maggi said nothing, waiting anxiously for him to continue.

"Do you remember a child star named Jackie Sommers?"

Maggi nodded slowly, not quite grasping what he had in mind. She didn't know why, but she felt a cold panic. A flood of memories returned.

Her first movie was supposed to have been a vehicle for Jackie Sommers. She remembered her mother hiding a newspaper article from her. Having her mother hide anything from her was so unusual that Maggi purposely pulled the paper out of the trash. She read about Jackie's suicide. Her mother was trying to shield her, to keep her from feeling that self-destruction was at the end of the road to stardom. She remembered how sad she had been, sad without fully comprehending the ramifications of the story. She had been twelve at the time.

A year later, she suffered the same fate that Jackie had. She was cut from the studio, from her lifeline. Except that she had had the presence of mind to survive. Maybe, she thought now, it had been due in part to that story she had read, the story about Jackie. She had vowed that something like that would never happen to her.

Brent! Was he related to Jackie? Was that why he had looked the way he had last night when they talked about Hollywood cast-offs? Did he know who she was? Why hadn't he said anything? That guarded look she saw, was that hate? Did he somehow blame her for all this?

"Then Brent is—"

"Jackie's brother," Norman finished for her.

"Oh, God, what a mess!" Maggi groaned.

"I was beginning to think you had been struck dumb," Norman said.

"Numb is more like it."

"What are you going to do?"

She stared at Norman for a long moment. *Do? What is there to do?*

Suddenly, she knew. She stood up. "Talk to him."

"It might not be wise. Maybe I should..." he began to offer.

A bittersweet smile flickered over Maggi's lips. "Wisdom and show people don't go hand in hand. If we were a wise lot, we'd be working steady jobs."

"Maggi." Norman took her hands into his. They felt ice-cold. "Are you going to be all right?"

"Sure, I'm a trooper," she said, lifting her chin for effect. "Besides, I'm not the one who had a brother who committed suicide."

Ethel came in, humming "Oh, What a Beautiful Morning."

"Try 'Stormy Weather,' Ethel," Maggi advised. "I think we're in for it."

SHE WAS GOING to play it by ear, to keep her emotions bottled up and let him talk. It all made sense now, his dislike of show business, the sad, pensive, perturbed look in his eyes, the penetrating stares. They all added up. He knew, knew who she was, had known all along. Then why hadn't he *said* anything? There had to be a reason.

Oh, God, she thought, did he blame her for what happened to his brother? Then why had he wanted to go to bed with her? she suddenly wondered. Had he made the proposition to get back at her somehow? To lead her on and then punish her? Her chest began to ache as pain filled her.

He hadn't been honest with her. Damn it, she would have bet her soul on his honesty.

Just shows what a rotten judge of character you are.

By the time she got to his office, she was a smoldering caldron of emotions about to erupt.

"Ms. Cole," Marietta barked sharply as Maggi stalked past her desk, "he's on the phone!"

"Well, he can damn well hang up!"

Maggi threw open the door, her own hurt rising like bile in her throat. Why did she have to be attracted to him of all people? With handsome men flocking in to tape the show, why did it have to be this man?

Brent was stunned by the look on her face. Her fine-boned features had been somber, whimsical, mischievous and tempting. But never had he seen her like this. Pain, anger and futile hope passed back and forth, none staying.

"I'll call you back," he said to the man on the phone and then hung up before he received an answer. "Maggi, what's wrong?"

"You tell me."

"This has gone too far. I am calling the security guard," Marietta threatened through the opened door. She yanked the phone from the cradle.

"You'll do no such thing!" Brent ordered, not looking in the woman's direction.

Marietta decided to type her letter of resignation. She wasn't up to this personal nonsense.

Brent closed the door behind Maggi slowly, uncertain of his next move. "What's on your mind, Maggi?"

Maggi struggled very hard to keep her accusation from spilling out. "Why haven't you arranged for a meeting with the committee?"

Was that what this was all about? Somehow, he didn't think so.

"These things take time, Maggi. Normally, you have to put your request in writing and then it takes months. In this case, I've waived the rules. But the committee doesn't just convene out of the blue. Two of the members are away. They'll be back within the week and then—"

"Why didn't you tell me?" she asked in a small, choked voice.

He looked at the tears shimmering in her eyes.

She knows.

He felt relieved. The charade was over. He crossed over to her and took her hands. "I was going to," he confessed. "I really wanted to. But I didn't know where or how to start."

Maggie pulled her hands back. She couldn't think when he touched her, couldn't focus her mind. Her professional outrage at being strung along warred with the hurt that she felt personally. She had been ready to let herself go, to love this man who looked so in need of loving, and all the time, he was stringing her along, waiting to pay her back, to use her.

"I don't believe you," she said quietly. "I think all you want is revenge."

He paused for a long moment. Finally, he answered her. "Yes."

Chapter Nine

"Well, I guess there isn't any more to say, is there?" Maggi's voice was brimming with emotion. Actually, there was a lot to say, but she was afraid that if she said any of it, she would start to cry and she didn't want to cry in front of him. That would only sweeten his revenge.

She turned to leave, but Brent caught her by the shoulders. The pressure of his fingers held her fast.

"Let me go, Brent. Let me go, or I swear I won't be held responsible for what I say," she threatened.

His eyes, twin mirrors of misery, swept over her face. "Don't go," he asked softly.

"Why?" she demanded. Her eyes shimmered with the tears she was holding back. "Is there a part two to your plan? Isn't it enough that you've tried to ruin the benefit, that you made me waste my time by leading me to believe you'd let me address the committee?"

"Maggi," he implored, "I need to talk to you."

She wanted to leave, to get out of there as fast as she could. She needed time to herself in order to pull the pieces together and think like a producer, not a woman. How could she salvage the show before financial ruin annihilated it? The part of her that ached, that hurt for the relationship she had hoped would flower, that part she would deal with later—two weeks later. By then, the pain wouldn't be so raw.

Maybe.

But there was something in his voice, something in his eyes, that kept her immobile. Maybe, somehow, things could be straightened out. Maybe it wasn't all so hopeless after all. Norman always said that the song about a cockeyed optimist in *South Pacific* was written about her. But still, she couldn't live without hope.

"All right," she agreed.

"Not here." He took her hand. "Let's go somewhere else, away from here. I don't want to talk about it in this office. Here the public Brent Sommerfield exists, works, is successful." The words sounded hollow when he said them.

"Then where?"

"Home." He reached for the door, but it was already opening from the outside.

Marietta was in such a hurry that for the first time in her life, she hadn't bothered to knock. Not only hadn't she knocked, but she almost collided with Brent and Maggi on their way out. Marietta took one step back, recovered and thrust an envelope toward Brent.

"Mr. Sommerfield, I'd like you to take this." Marietta looked right through Maggi.

"Not now, Marietta." His voice was tight, controlled.

Marietta might not have been aware of the tumultuous emotions just beneath the surface, but Maggi was. She could sense them. He couldn't have been out just for revenge. He *couldn't* have been, she insisted, trying to calm her raw nerves.

Brent brushed the envelope aside as he walked out. "I'm taking the rest of the afternoon off."

"The rest of the . . . ?" Marietta couldn't finish her statement. She was too stunned. If she had harbored any last-minute doubts, this convinced her. The woman had gotten to him. Brent Sommerfield had been the embodiment of the work ethic that was so important to her, and now he had been transformed into a womanizer just like her other bosses. The Brent Sommerfield she had originally come to work for would never have left the office in the middle of the day for personal reasons. And this was only the beginning. Soon, the little games would begin, just as they had with her other bosses.

Marietta marched into his office to place her letter of resignation on his desk.

"WHERE ARE WE GOING?" Maggi asked as they walked down the block. He held her firmly by the hand. If she had any thoughts about getting away, she couldn't readily do so without causing a scene.

"My apartment."

Then why weren't they taking the limousine?

Questions flashed through her mind. She had to wait. Once they were alone, he'd sort it all out for her. He had to.

He was silent on the walk there. She let him maintain his peace, her own mind partially numb. What was she going to do if, after he told his story, he still refused to let her go to the committee? Maybe she could talk the creditors into underwriting the balance. Tell them how good this would look on their income tax forms at tax time. Maybe she could get Norman to...

Hope did not spring eternal, but at least she was thinking again, she told herself. Thinking about work while physically linked to a man who hated her.

No, that wasn't hate she saw in his eyes, she argued. But now that the truth was out, she could give meaning to the strange looks she had seen on his face. He had been plotting his revenge from the very moment she had so "cleverly" managed to gain access to his office.

"Why didn't we take the limousine?" Her legs ached from keeping up with his long stride.

"I need to walk."

Was he trying to compose himself? His composure had dropped for a moment back there in his office. Was he now trying to regain it so that he could calmly relate his story, make all his points neatly as if he were at a board meeting? She stifled the desire to break free. *Hear him out, Maggi. The war isn't lost yet.*

They hurried through the diamond district. Thousands of gems caught the bright morning sun as it shone down, warming the lifeless stones, making them seem alive. Store owners stood in doorways, waiting to entice prospective customers. People lined the glitter-filled storefronts, window shopping. But Maggi scarcely noticed any of it. She was too concerned with the man who grasped her hand so tightly and led her down the crowded street.

The back of her legs ached by the time they reached his apartment.

"Mr. Sommerfield," Saunders gasped when Brent let himself in. The valet's glance took in Maggi, then swept back to his employer. "Is anything wrong?"

"Take the afternoon off, Saunders," Brent ordered without breaking stride as he walked into the living room.

Saunders stared after him, stunned. Mr. Sommerfield never came home early. But it was not his position to wonder. Quietly, Saunders took his jacket and left.

"Well, I've lost three pounds jogging after you for fifteen blocks. Are you ready to talk, or is there more to this confessional ritual?" She knew she didn't sound very reasonable and was glad of it, since reasonable was the last thing she wanted to be. She felt betrayed. The man she was beginning to care for deeply, the man she had almost gone to bed with, had been using her as an instrument for his own personal revenge against the acting community. That didn't exactly arouse tender, understanding feelings.

"Yes, I'm ready to talk."

"All right." She steeled herself and sat down on the circular sofa, perching on the very edge of the cushion, her body rigid. She knew she wasn't going to be happy with what she was about to hear. "Talk."

Brent sat down next to her. It was a different Brent, far less formal, far less in control of the situation. It was as if a secret door were slowly opening, revealing an unknown Brent, a vulnerable Brent.

He cleared his throat, then looked at her a bit ruefully. "I have no idea where to begin," he confessed.

"At the beginning would be nice," she said, trying to keep her own emotions in check.

"Ah, in the beginning," he said slowly, "in the beginning it was all wonderful. Endless parties, people fawning, servants, laughter. Jackie was the center of a wonderful universe." There was a deep affection in his voice.

As she watched him, she could see by the look on his face that for a brief moment, he was reliving the past. The corners of his mouth had softened as he mentioned his brother's name. He had loved Jackie very much, of that she was certain. But how had that love infused hatred within the man who sat next to her?

She went on listening.

He turned to look at Maggi. "When he lost that last part to you, it was the beginning of the end." He honestly didn't mean for it to sound accusing, but it did.

Then she knew everything. It wasn't the acting community he blamed; it was Maggi. She opened her mouth to defend herself, but for the first time in her life she was speechless. With this revelation, the situation had evolved into something totally unreal, something she didn't know how to deal with. She forced herself to go on listening. The more she knew, the better she could organize her defense. And she knew with all her heart that she intended to mount a defense.

"No one would hire him anymore. He wasn't right for anything. They wanted either child stars or adult actors. He was locked in limbo between the two. At fourteen, he was a has-been."

She remembered the way she had felt when the door had slammed in her face. *I was one at thirteen. He had one more year than I had.*

Brent looked down at his hands. "We had to move out of the mansion we were living in." He sighed as he vividly recollected the packing, the recriminations. "Had to move out of a lot of places after that. There never seemed to be any money to pay the rent, no matter how small the rent became." The smile that touched his lips was now bitter. He got up, as if the memories were too difficult to deal with while he was seated.

"She liked to spend money, my mother. Liked the prestige of being Jackie Sommers's mother. I don't think she ever forgave him for letting her lose that. Not him, or you." Brent turned to look at Maggi. For the last time, he searched his heart for the hatred his mother had tried to instill in him. It wasn't there. When face to face with her, he couldn't hate Maggi, not for their fate, not for his brother's death. Not even though he had tried. He didn't know what he felt anymore. A piece of him, a piece of the incredible mosaic that had gone into making his young life, was missing.

"My mother hated you."

It felt like a wave hitting her. A tall, oppressive wave. "But I—" Maggi nearly gasped out in self-defense.

Brent shook his head, cutting her short. "You took his place on the lot. That was all my mother remembered. You were the new reigning darling and Jackie, at fourteen, was no one's *Little Darling*," he said bitterly, recalling the name of the movie. "He took it very hard," Brent went on, walking toward her. "He was never quite so alive as he was when he stood on a soundstage, pretending to be someone else. He didn't want to be Jackie Sommerfield. He wanted to be Jackie Sommers. He wanted the make-believe, the fanfare. I don't think he ever really liked himself." A bitter look entered his eyes. "And my mother didn't help. Day in, day out, she kept after him, telling him that he was a failure, that if he had any gumption he would talk the studio bosses into letting him back on a picture, any picture. She never realized that he wasn't capable of fighting fights like that. She was, and God knows she tried." He laughed shortly, shoving his clenched hands into his pockets. "She got herself escorted off more than one studio lot. And it all came back to hating you." He looked at Maggi again. "She blamed you for everything."

Maggi's stomach churned. A protest rose in her throat, but she stilled it, waiting for him to finish.

"After...after Jackie killed himself, I went on to try to piece together my own life as best I could. As I grew older, I knew that if I let the venom my mother was spewing get to me, I would be as lost as Jackie was. I was determined to escape, to make something of myself, recapture a lot of the so-called good life. I wanted it more for Jackie's sake than my own.

"But nothing I ever did was good enough. After his death, Mother enshrined Jackie in her mind, forgetting all the recriminations she had heaped on him when he was alive. Suddenly, he became the saint and you the sinner. I guess she had to do that for her own peace of mind. Pretty soon, she began blaming you for his death, just as she had blamed you for his failure. I don't think she was ever quite right after that. She died blaming you for her lot in life. By then I had become rather wealthy," he said, his voice hollow. "I just went on with my life, pushing the past as far away as I could.

"Until you showed up in my life." His eyes held her captive as he finished his story. "You brought it all back, all the bitterness I felt when Jackie died. I'm not quite sure what came over me, but I felt I had to pay you back a little for all the grief we had gone through." He saw her start to say something and he put his hand on her face, cupping it gently. "You have to understand that all these feelings, childish though they may seem, *began* in childhood, were instilled in childhood. It's hard to shake something like that." He let her go. "But the more I grew to know you, the more I realized how futile seeking revenge was, how pointless."

"But I didn't have anything to do with it," she insisted. "The star system got me, too. Got me when I was a year younger than your brother. I was thirteen when they let me go, telling me that I was too gangly to cast in anything."

"Thirteen?" he echoed, not really understanding her.

"Thirteen. Your brother didn't have a patent on rejection. A lot of us got it. It's the public's fault, if you must blame someone. The same public that fawns on you and makes you feel like a god. Their tastes change, they fall in and out of love with heroes and heroines, children and character actors. Millions of dollars are spent each year, trying to second-guess the public's reactions, and no one can do it a hundred percent of the time. Your brother and I were fortunate enough to grab a little of the stardust for a while. A lot of kids found their hours of dance and voice lessons coming to nothing but endless frustration."

For a moment, the sound of her voice hung in the air, then faded, leaving an unsettling quiet.

Brent took a deep breath. "I really, really loved him. But I couldn't save him, couldn't help him pull his life together."

There it was, all the raw pain, all the guilt he had carried with him all these years, guilt wrapped in a young boy's tender heart. He had been incapable of saving the one person he loved, and it tore him apart.

"Oh, Brent," Maggi whispered. She rose and put her arms around him, wanting to absorb some of his pain. "I'm so sorry." She kissed him tenderly on the cheek, aching for him, aching for Jackie and all the Jackies of the world.

Somehow, with a movement that was barely perceptible, the kiss on his cheek became one on the lips. Followed by another, and another. A torrent of dammed feelings broke loose for both of them. His vulnerability had weakened his restraint.

Brent pulled her into his arms and kissed her so hard that it startled her. It awakened her own repressed feelings, feelings she had tried to hold back the other night. Love, desire, compassion all mixed wildly together in an emotional storm she had no control over. She clung to him as the pressure of his mouth grew more and more intense, burning her, stripping her of everything but her need for him.

It seemed to her that his warm, enticing mouth was everywhere at once, draining her of her tranquillity and filling her with a wonder that she found hard to describe. Bathed in the cathartic aura of her understanding, Brent kissed her cheeks, her eyes, her forehead, assaulting her lips and her senses at the same time. She found herself surrounded by a sea of desire.

"Oh, God, Maggi, you make me feel whole again," he whispered against the hollow of her throat, his warm breath curling against her skin. She clung to him as he framed her neck with kisses. He opened the first button of her blouse. And then he stopped.

Surprised, she looked into his eyes, wondering what had happened.

"Maggi, am I going too fast for you?"

The display of gentleness at a moment like this entirely undid her. She moved her hand to the second button and opened it for him. "No," she whispered, "not too fast."

It was all the encouragement he needed. The blouse parted swiftly, revealing a cream-colored bra that acted as a barrier for only a fraction of a moment. His hand slid along her back, pressing her to him. He separated the clasp as his mouth once more took possession of hers. The almost savage need she had felt in his kiss had abated, to be replaced by kisses that were no less urgent, but gentler. His control over his passions had returned, not to divorce him from the situation but to enable him to heighten them with a slow, deliberate progression.

Maggi felt the bra leave her breasts as his fingers slid over the tender skin, stroking her softly. She felt the ache within her breasts grow instantly. Maggi wanted more, wanted to feel the sweet touch of his mouth on them. It was incredible. It was as if she were experiencing strong, physical needs for the very first time. Her marriage bed lay so far in the past and there had been almost nothing since, certainly not the passionate desire that was seizing her now.

Without realizing it, she buried her hands in the silken abundance of his raven hair and urged his head down ever so gently. A trail of kisses wound its way down from her mouth, to her chin, to the pulsating hollow of her throat. They all echoed the demanding rhythm growing between her thighs. Slowly, his lips moved down to her breasts. Moist kisses encircled one aching tip, and then the other. Maggi felt her mind swirling away. A last cry of warning echoed in her brain. This could be his last attempt at revenge, to render her almost mindless with passion, and then desert her. But if that was what he intended, his goal had already been reached. All she could think of, all she wanted, was to touch him, to feel him against her, to have him want her, for whatever reason. Later, she'd deal with all this rationally. For the moment, she was totally devoid of rationality. She was a symphony of passion, nothing less, nothing more.

The blouse dropped from her shoulders and Brent covered every exposed inch with a throbbing blanket of kisses, gently massaging the aching mounds of her breasts over and over.

In a warm, wonderful haze, Maggi began to unbutton his shirt. She wanted to touch his chest, wanted to run her hands along his smooth, hard skin, wanted to possess him by touch as much as he possessed her.

He drew back from her, then gently put her hands at her sides. "I'll do it," he offered.

"No," she said, "let me."

His hands dropped from his jacket and he smiled invitingly at her. His face was softer than she had ever seen it, softer and kinder. It was as if something had been purged from his soul. Maggi quickly removed his jacket, slid off his tie and undid the buttons of his shirt, pulling the tails out of his trousers.

"Better?" he asked.

She merely nodded, incapable of forming words. When she had seen him the other day in the gym, his form-fitting pullover had hinted at the sculptured proportions of his chest and arms. Seeing him naked from the waist up made her catch her breath. He was magnificent.

"My turn," he whispered softly.

His hands were at her waist, spanning it, then his fingers slipped beneath the waistband. Torrid emotions surged through her, needs blossomed within her, threatening to swallow her up. She had never felt anything so all-consuming before.

His fingers brushed deftly along the rim of the skirt. The skirt skimmed down her warm, wanting thighs, guided by his hands, his wonderful hands that were evoking magic wherever he touched. Within seconds, she was standing before him in only her silk panties. She had never been next to him without her shoes; now she found she only came up to his chin.

Raising herself on her toes, she kissed his throat, her tongue flicked lightly along his Adam's apple as her hands, soft and teasing, traced the pattern of muscles along his chest. There was a slight quiver in response as her fingertips lightly touched here and there.

She heard him whisper her name softly. There was a wanting in his voice, a wanting so great that it stirred her passion to a near frenzy.

Suddenly, she felt herself being lifted up into strong arms, lifted and carried. A shower of copper fell over his arm as Maggi rested her head against his shoulder, her arms about his neck.

She was wrong. He *was* Rhett to her Scarlett.

Chapter Ten

No, she wouldn't be Scarlett for him, Maggi thought as he carried her into his bedroom. She'd be different. She'd never do anything to make him say he didn't give a damn about her.

She took note of his bedroom, it was restrained, but dynamic. It reflected him totally. She could feel his heart vibrating against her body just before he gently placed her on the bed. He looked down at her, making her think of a dark, brooding Heathcliff—Laurence Olivier at his most handsome. She had always had a soft spot for Olivier.

"I never thought I'd want to make love to Maggi McCree." The words were uttered incredulously. A small portion of him was still given up to guilt. He was actually holding her, holding Maggi McCree in his arms. Maggi McCree, the person his brother had blamed so bitterly for his fate. He shouldn't be doing this; it was crazy. And yet, he wanted her, wanted her more than he had ever wanted any other woman. He couldn't help himself.

Maggi lifted her arms toward him. The invitation was there in her eyes. He took her into his arms with gentle reverence, as if he couldn't believe any of this was happening.

"You're not. Maggi McCree is a little girl who lives on film in some dusty studio vault. I'm just Maggi," she whispered, her voice husky with desire. *Your Maggi if you want me.*

He responded with a kiss, a feathery light kiss that nearly drove her wild.

Had anyone ever felt this way before? Had anyone ever wanted another human being the way she wanted him? This was what it was all about, this was love in Technicolor, in Cinemascope. It surrounded her like the giant movie screens of yesteryear. This was what she had once thought she was going to have with Johnny, but that had dissolved into a series of warm meetings of the body. This, this was something entirely different. This was a meeting of souls, of passions, of needs.

He withdrew from her and Maggi felt the absence throughout her entire being. Had he, at the very last minute, changed his mind? Was he bringing her to the very brink of passion only to leave her alone?

Her look of apprehension softened as she saw him shed the rest of his clothes in swift, fluid motions. His eyes never left her body. He was making love to her without touching her.

As the last bit of fabric left his body, Maggi looked on with unabashed admiration. She didn't have to say a word. It was all there in her eyes.

Brent slid down next to her, and the warmth of his body radiated against her own, thrilling her, making her pulse go wild.

"Don't you think we should get rid of these?" He ran his finger teasingly along the perimeter of her panties.

"It would make things easier." She was astounded that she could sound so light and nonchalant when her body fairly cried out for him.

His hands began stroking her, caressing her, arousing her as he touched every part of her, moving with a sureness that bespoke deep intimacy. Slowly, her underwear was coaxed down, slipping along her thighs until it slid onto the floor beyond his bed.

Their bodies grew closer still, laced together with passion. He rolled onto her, pressing her beneath him. She could feel the full measure of his desire as the hard ridges of his body imprinted themselves on hers.

And still he held himself back.

What did he want from her? What type of surrender was he demanding? Her long lashes fluttered up as she stared at him. Why was he waiting?

"Love me, Brent," she whispered.

He swept the hair from her face, his eyes tender as he regarded her. "I fully intend to."

"Say my name," she asked.

"Maggi."

"Again." She needed to hear it without any blame, without a trace of anything but the desire she felt so flush against her.

"Maggi." This time, it was a groan, rippling from his chest against hers. "Beautiful, wonderful Maggi." His mouth found hers again.

When their bodies finally joined together as one continuous whole, Maggi thought she had reached the very brink of sanity. Beyond sanity lay a wonderland that nothing had ever prepared her for. All the magic, all the wonders of the world paled before this feeling of ecstasy, the feeling of fulfillment she experienced.

They were breathless as they floated together into contentment. She could feel the sweat of his body mingling with her own, could feel the weight of his body as it pressed against hers, spent. But when he moved to withdraw from her, she murmured a protest, wanting to feel him there just a little longer, wanting to be part of him just a moment more. He cradled her against him, and she felt him relax.

Now, God, if I'm to die, make it now. It can't get any better than this.

She reached over and secured a corner of the bedspread. As she moved to cover herself, Brent stopped her.

"No, not yet. Let me look at you."

His words made her smile and she snuggled against him. "Go ahead, I'm used to being stared at."

"Like this?" he asked, running a hand along the long line of her thigh.

She stirred beneath his hand. "No, not exactly like this," she conceded with a grin.

"You put the most wanton thoughts into my head," he murmured, his breath tickling her shoulder.

"That's what you get for hanging around show people." She laughed as she raised herself on one elbow. "Tell me about your thoughts," she urged. Her eyes devoured the splendid visual feast his body presented. "Maybe we can do something about them."

"Right now," he confessed, "I don't think I could do anything about it if the bed were on fire."

"Oh?"

He saw the teasing look that came into her eyes.

"Too tired?" she cooed.

"Exhausted."

"Well, then I guess there's no harm in my doing this." She bent her head and nibbled on his ear. He shivered in response. "And you probably wouldn't even notice if I let my hand do a little wandering."

"Wandering?" He arched a brow as she began to move her hand in a tiny circle along his lightly haired chest.

"Yes. Wandering. Exploring. Famillarizing myself with terrain I've just been introduced to." She tried to keep her voice detached but she was having a hard time.

He was having an even harder one, she noted with glee. Her hand moved to his waist and they both knew she wasn't about to stop there.

"Yup, I guess you're dead-tired," she said, her voice growing sensuously low. "Well," she reconsidered, "maybe not so dead." She was getting a definite reaction, she thought, as she ran her fingers along his thigh, her forearm just barely touching his most intimate feature.

She watched his face intently, seeing the way his muscles tightened ever so slightly as her fingers curled taking possession of him, her palm stroking him as gently as his had stroked her breast.

"Maggi." His voice was strangled with swiftly mounting desire.

"What," she cried innocently, "not tired anymore?"

He grabbed her forearms and with a neat twist, he positioned her beneath him again, her hair framed out like a copper halo. But she had done things to him no angel would have dreamed of.

"Maggi, you could raise the dead," he told her, his mouth inches away from hers.

"I'll settle for you," she told him, crossing her wrists behind his head and pulling him closer to her. "I'll definitely settle for you."

"NORMAN MUST BE FRANTIC," Maggi said, slipping on her clothes. "I was supposed to go over the final version of the taping with him an hour ago." She grinned at Brent ruefully, watching as he slid his trousers up his muscular legs. A tingle of desire came over her. *My God, are you never satisfied?* "I've never done anything like this before."

"Been late, you mean?" Brent asked.

"Among other things," she said vaguely, buttoning her blouse.

He came up behind her, drawing her against his chest and dropping a light kiss against her ear. A deep whiff of her perfume floated through his senses. He had come to love jasmine in the past few hours.

"What other things?" he prodded, marveling at the way he felt. It was as if an immense burden had been lifted from him. He felt alive, like a new man, totally reborn. Would it fade? God, he hoped not.

Maggi turned within the small circle of his arms until she was looking up into his eyes. "Never made wild, passionate love in the afternoon to someone who spent his life hating me." She searched his face. Her expression grew serious. "Do you? Do you still feel that way about me?"

Slowly, he shook his head. "I could never feel anything but . . . what I do for you."

At the last moment, he hesitated. Love was a particularly difficult word for him. It never entered his vocabulary. Perhaps all he was feeling was a mixture of relief and physical longing. She was the most attractive woman he had ever held in his arms. Let it rest at that for now.

But Maggi didn't want it to rest. "Which is?" she prodded.

"You left your shoes under the coffee table." Brent walked out of the room.

"Coward," Maggi whispered affectionately. A smile played on her lips. She followed him into the other room. "Shoes were the last thing on my mind when I stood here before," Maggi informed him. She rested one hand on his shoulder as she slipped first one foot and then the another into her shoes.

He returned her smile. "I'll have Digby drop you off at your office, if that's what you'd like," he offered.

No, that's not what I'd like. I'd like to stay here with you, in your bed, until I'm wrinkled and old and they have to pry me away from you.

What she said was, "Digby is probably sitting around, wondering what happened to you. We left him back at your office, remember? You did a brooding Marlon Brando act for fifteen blocks."

It came back to him. "Oh, that's right. All right, I'll have the doorman call us a cab and we can both get back to work."

"Right, business as usual," she said crisply. They both knew it was a sham.

He pulled her into his arms. "When can I see you again?"

"Anytime you please."

"Tonight."

She frowned, thinking of the mess on her desk. "I should be burning the midnight oil after this afternoon—"

"Conservation is still in vogue, so they tell me. Save the oil, come back with me tonight."

"What will Saunders say?" she teased, wrapping her arms around his back.

"Saunders does not say anything, madam. Saunders merely serves." The valet had returned and surprised them both by silently entering the room. "Will there be two for dinner, sir?"

"Two?" Brent asked, looking at Maggi.

"Two." She buried her head against his chest. It smelled of cologne, with a faint trace of her perfume mingled in. God, she felt wonderful!

"Saunders," Brent said, walking toward the door with his arm around Maggi's shoulders, "It occurs to me that I've been working you too hard. You deserve the weekend off."

"The whole weekend, sir?" Saunders asked, amazed as he looked at Maggi. In his entire service with the man, he had seen two, perhaps three, women stay the night. None had ever returned. It was as if Mr. Sommerfield went out of his way not to form attachments. Certainly none had ever lasted more than one day.

Brent looked at Maggi, thinking of her as some kind of rare magic that had been visited upon him. "The whole weekend."

Maggi bit her lip uncertainly. There were so many ends to tie up before Monday. "Brent, I don't know—"

He bent his head and kissed her lips lightly. "The whole weekend."

There was no arguing with his tone. "Well, you kissed me in front of Saunders. I guess that makes it official." She winked at Saunders. "The whole weekend," she agreed.

"MY GOD, MAGGI, where have you been?" Norman cried when she walked in. "I was ready to call the police, except they don't even look for their own mothers until they've been declared missing for twenty-four hours."

Maggi gave the round little man a broad, satisfied smile. She couldn't get her mind into gear quite yet. "Oz, Shangri-la, Bali-Ha'i, Xanadu, take your pick." She more or less poured herself into her chair. Her entire body was fluid.

Norman stared at her. She was acting crazy. "Maggi, it's not like you to run out in the middle of the day. I know you were upset, but think of what you left behind," he cried. The past four hours had been hell. Maggi was always the peacemaker, the one who could be relied on to smooth out any storm. He had depended on her for so long that he had been lost without her. "Blankenship is demanding another audition. Says he can't find the right—" He stopped. "Are you listening to me?"

Maggi nodded. She was staring at him, or rather, she appeared to be looking right through him. She hadn't heard a word, he thought. Norman's worst fears were confirmed. "He made love to you, didn't he?"

She deliberately didn't answer him. Instead, she pretended to be shocked. "Norman, do I ask you about what you do on your own time?"

"This wasn't your own time and my life is an open book." Maggi fixed him with a recriminating look. "A dull, open book with a few missing pages. But you, you're a babe in the woods."

"I come from the woods of Hollywood," she pointed out, tickled with his concern.

"And how you reached the age of thirty-eight—"

"Thirty-five."

"...without being eaten alive is beyond me. I want to know what happened." He dragged a chair over. The pile of papers the chair had supported toppled immediately and spread across the floor like a broken fan. He didn't even notice. "What did he do to you?"

Maggi knew it was concern rather than anything else that drove him on. She rather liked having someone worry about her, she thought. And Norman was like a father to her. She rose, patting his shoulder. "I don't think you're old enough to hear this."

Norman pretended to bury his head in his hands. "Baby's all grown up now. I liked you better as Audrey Hepburn's understudy in *The Nun's Story*," he quipped. Then the kidding stopped. "Did you talk about his brother?"

"Yes."

"And?"

"Seems both his brother and his mother blamed me for the end of Jackie's career."

Norman rose to his feet, his hands unconsciously clenched at his sides. "That's crazy. You?'

Maggi kissed the top of Norman's head. "Down, great protector. I guess they had to blame somebody. Anyway, no harm's done. Brent doesn't blame me."

"He said so, I take it."

No, she realized, *he hadn't.* Now, away from the warmth of his mouth, the heat of his body, it left a small, gnawing doubt that she pushed aside. "Not in so many words, but he said he didn't hate me."

"Swell," Norman muttered sarcastically. He didn't like the way this was going. "How about the money for the benefit?"

Maggi looked away. Another omission. "We didn't talk about that."

Norman lifted her chin and looked at her closely. "Small wonder. Your lips look as if they've been permanently pressed. Take my advice, Maggi, leave your heart out of this. You're too good to waste on a stuffed shirt."

"I think," she said dreamily, "that he's been permanently unstuffed."

"Worse than I thought," Norman said to the chair. "She's gone off the deep end."

"Not so gone," Maggi laughed, snapping out of her reverie. "We've still got a show to put on."

"If your boyfriend ever decides to let you talk to the money people."

"He will, Norman. He will."

Norman wished he could be as sure as Maggi, but he had a nagging feeling that she was being used.

"I WARNED YOU about midnight oil," Brent said as he walked into the room. It was close to eight o'clock. "I had a hell of a time getting in. The security guard downstairs thought I was some stagestruck fan of Lorna Lang's."

"Lauren Lang's," Maggi corrected. "She's flown in a week early to start rehearsals on her dance number," she told him without looking up. It was in self-defense. She wanted to finish working on some notes

to the costume designer before she left and she knew
if she looked up, the notes would be abandoned.
"She's gotten six calls from a very passionate admirer
in the past two days alone. She's one of the new golden
girls in Hollywood, poor thing. Doesn't realize yet that
she's only riding the crest of a wave. As soon as you hit
a certain magic number, you're not a golden girl anymore. You're a fledgling character actress."

He took the pen out of her hand.

Maggi's head jerked up. "Hey, I'm not through
yet."

"Yes you are," he said firmly, pocketing the pen. "I
promised Digby he could get off early tonight. That
means you have to cooperate."

"Okay," she agreed. "I know when I'm licked.
We'll just stop at the hotel—"

"No time."

"But what'll I wear tonight?"

"Me."

The proposition sounded most intriguing from
where she stood. A twinkle entered her eye. "Well, if
you insist."

He took her hand firmly in his. "I insist."

This time it was Maggi who hummed "Some Enchanted Evening" as she left the office. Too bad Ethel
wasn't around, she thought, to take notes.

Chapter Eleven

Brent scarcely knew himself. He was like a man who'd had a blindfold removed for the first time. The world wasn't dark, it was filled with colors, beautiful, radiant colors and Maggi had done it for him.

He smiled warmly at her and drew her close as they rode back to his apartment. She had given him a new beginning. It was as if he had suddenly been given the youth he had never had. Life had been much too serious ever to laugh after Jackie was gone. Now, Brent felt a smile encompassing his entire being.

How could he ever have entertained the idea that she was to blame for what had happened? Maggi could never do anything to hurt anyone. It was the industry she was involved with, that was to blame for destroying hearts and dreams. He wished she wasn't part of it.

Brent put the thought out of his mind. This weekend there was to be no thought of that, no thought of anything but the woman fate had been kind enough to send into his two-dimensional life. He couldn't let himself spoil it by examining the feelings that were not totally resolved yet.

"I really shouldn't be doing this, you know," Maggi said. She leaned her head against his shoulder.

"Yes, you should."

She could feel the words as they rumbled in his chest and she loved it. She pressed her hand against his chest, toying with the buttons on his shirt. "There's just a ton of things I should be tending to. The stars begin arriving on Monday. So many of them want to incorporate minivacations with their appearance, and they expect someone to dance in attendance to them. Things'll really start to get hectic then. I'm going to be twice as busy. I was planning on catching up this weekend before they got here."

"Plans have a way of being changed. The best laid plans—"

"Of mice and men," she concluded. "Yes, I know, I know." She sighed as she twisted one button open, then another. Slowly, she slipped her hand in. Ever so lightly, she rubbed her fingertips along the hard ridges of his chest, teasing the hairs. She was arousing him, she could tell by the look in his eyes and the deep, satisfied smile on his lips.

Maggi Cole, producer, newly created femme fatale. It had a nice ring to it. She laughed softly.

"What's so funny?" He kissed the top of her head. She felt so good against him, so warm, so right.

"All this. I just set out to unstuff you, not to, well, you know."

"Consider me unstuffed," he said. He ran his hand along her jawline, tilting her head back until her lips offered themselves up to his. He kissed her lightly, not trusting himself to do anything else.

"Definitely unstuffed," Maggi murmured against his mouth as their lips parted. She caught sight of St. Patrick's Cathedral as they drove by. "I wonder if the candles did it?" she mused softly to herself.

"What?"

She shook her head. "Nothing, I was just thinking out loud."

Digby dropped them off in front of Brent's apartment. They were alone. In the heart of Manhattan, they were all alone. Anticipation enveloped her body. She really didn't have time for this, she admonished herself. She was supposed to be hard at work. She was supposed to be...right where she was. Maggi couldn't remember when she had felt so happy. They rode up in the elevator in contented silence.

You're wrong, Noël Coward, life doesn't begin at forty. It begins at thirty-five.

Brent closed the door behind them. How could such a simple gesture be so intimate? she wondered. She felt sealed off from the world, sealed to him, experiencing all the hopes, all the expectations of an excited young bride. The novelty of the idea struck her and she started to laugh at herself. She felt him behind her, then deliberately, he turned her around. His lips covered hers in a kiss that was deep and penetrating, a kiss that melted away all her thoughts. Her response was immediate.

Hungrily, with a passion that surprised not only Maggi but Brent as well, he showered her with tiny delicate kisses. With each pass of his lips, his intensity heightened.

"Was it something I said?" Maggi asked teasingly.

Brent shook his head and laughed. He loved her unpredictability. Maggi saw her fate in the shining mirrors of his eyes and her soul rushed out to meet it.

Kissing her neck ever so lightly, Brent's lips touched first one side and then the other. He hesitated for a moment. It took all her control not to reach out and pull him against her. Her whole body ached for him like an unfolding flower waiting for the first touch of the morning sun. A barrage of kisses trickled slowly down to her collarbone and Maggi could feel her heart pounding.

The chandelier above cast silvery threads of light about them. They seemed to mingle with the threads of undeniable desire Brent was creating inside her.

An eternity later, Brent answered the question she had forgotten to ask. "It's everything you've said," he whispered softly into her ear. "And everything you've done."

"You get turned on so easily," Maggi managed to say, losing herself to her consuming passion.

His sultry eyes looked down at her as he lifted his head for a moment. "No," he said quietly, "as a matter of fact, I don't."

She believed him. Maybe it was the oldest line in the world, but she believed him, heaven help her. *Mine. That makes you mine.*

"I want to know...everything about...you." Maggi
wanted to know every part of him, wanted to make
him hers, body and soul.

Brent swept her up into his arms and turned toward
his bedroom. "I am," he told her, stealing another
kiss along her neck, "actually a very single-minded
person. I believe in doing one thing at a time." He
paused to kiss her again and he felt her shiver in his
arms, a reaction that served only to increase his passion. "When I was a child," he went on, "I'd eat my
peas first, then my potatoes, then I'd turn my attention to the meat."

"Speaking of that," Maggi said, finally managing
to breathe properly, "we haven't had dinner yet."

"Hungry?"

"Yes," she breathed, looking at him intently.

"Good, we'll start with dessert." His eyes skimmed
over her fair complexion. "French vanilla. I've always loved French vanilla," he confided, breathing the
words against the sensitive area of her neck.

Maggi laughed, her head swimming with joy, with
desire, with love. "I'm not as fluffy as that," she
protested lightly.

"No," he agreed, "but just as delectable."

He pushed open his bedroom door with his shoulder, then set her down, allowing the length of her body
to slide along his as he did so. Every fiber in her being
was alerted to the powerful, hard composition of his
muscular frame.

"Wonderfully delectable," he repeated.

Maggi smiled, radiant, her eyes never leaving his. They made her feel more intoxicated than any drink she had ever had. "I don't know what to say," she answered. No one had ever said things to her the way he did.

"Say yes." His lips brushed against the rounded corners of each shoulder through her blouse.

"To what?" She was confused.

"To me." Brent slid one sleeve from her shoulder and then the other.

SHE FELL ASLEEP in his arms, content. There was no outside world, no benefit, no pressing bills. There was no board that he had not yet allowed her to see. There was nothing and no one, except for Brent.

Sleep did not come for Brent. He lay, holding her against him, stroking her hair and wondering if the newfound happiness that had overtaken him would last, or if it was all destined to be taken away from him, just as his happiness had that first time. Once again, his emotional world was centering on someone tied to show business. It made him feel insecure.

He wondered if she would be willing to give it all up for him. He wondered if he could bear her rejection if she refused. He pulled her closer to him.

"Hmm?" she murmured sleepily. "Is it time to get up already?"

"No, it's the middle of the night."

Maggi's eyes opened. For a fraction of a second, the sound of a voice answering her own disoriented her.

Then she remembered everything. She smiled and reached up to him, bringing his face down to her own.

"Again?" he asked, feeling her growing warm and supple against him.

She nodded dreamily. "Rehearsals are a very important part of my world."

"Rehearsal?" he echoed with a laugh. "I thought we had it down pat."

"Overconfidence is a very dangerous thing." She grinned. "Let's do it again, just to make sure we've got it right."

"I can see that you're a hard taskmaster," he said fondly.

"The hardest."

It was the last thing that was said for a long, long time as Maggi surrendered herself to the wonderful feeling that rose, full-grown, within her.

Brent put his doubts on hold as he went on to make love to Maggi to the fullest capacity either one of them had ever known.

FOR MAGGI, the weekend was a little bit of heaven tucked inside the whirlwind of activity that had surrounded her lately. Having left all the details for the show in Norman's hands, she divested her mind of everything but the man she was with. She found joy in doing the simplest of things for him, like making breakfast.

"I'm a fair hand at cooking, I'll have you know." Maggi waved a spatula at him when he teased her about her culinary abilities.

"You've a fairer hand at something else." He came up behind her and wrapped his arms around her middle. She was wearing one of his shirts, the shirttails coming down to her knees. And that was all. He felt himself becoming aroused again even as the smell of bacon wafted through the air. "I've never seen my shirt look so good." He kissed her neck.

"If you don't eat—" she grinned "—you won't have any energy."

He traced the outline of her ear with his tongue, making her shiver. "You'll find a way to bring it out for me."

She had the presence of mind to turn off the stove.

And so it went the whole weekend. They took long walks and made love. Tried to watch television and made love. Talked and made love.

HER WEEKEND WAS, Maggi thought on Monday morning as the din and the details of the extravaganza threatened to swallow her up, the real stuff that dreams are made of. Hollywood was a poor second. But it was Hollywood that was demanding her attention now.

"I hope you rested well this weekend," Norman said sarcastically when she arrived late. She was more than a little surprised to see him in that early. He looked tired and she felt a slight pang of guilt at having left him alone to tend to all this. He was, in his own way, as much of a perfectionist as she was. As far as she knew, she had been the only one to whom he had ever delegated his responsibilities. "Because all hell broke loose here."

Maggi deposited her purse in the bottom drawer and shut the drawer with her foot. "Norman, it's only been two days, and the weekend on top of that. What could have happened?" Nothing was going to spoil her mood, nothing.

"What could have happened? he asked wearily, his voice going up an octave."Do you really want to know? Mr. Soft-shoe is threatening to pack up and go home."

Maggi had to stop and think for a moment before she remembered that Mr. Soft-shoe was what Norman called Blankenship. At least that was the way he referred to him in front of her. She knew he had another name for the choreographer in private.

Damn that man and his gargantuan ego. "Why?"

"Because I told him his number couldn't run longer than seven minutes. He wants twelve."

Ethel chose that moment to bring in the coffee. The tune for the morning was "I'm Gonna Wash That Man Right Out-a My Hair." It took a bit of doing to recognize it.

Maggi reached for her cup and absorbed the warmth between her hands before she ventured to take a sip. Ethel's coffee felt better than it tasted.

Ethel's song brought another thought to Norman's mind, a thought even more pressing than the benefit. "Are you?" Norman asked.

Had she missed something? "Am I what?"

Norman nodded toward the departed secretary. "Are you going to wash him out of your hair? Did the weekend get him out of your system?"

Maggi merely smiled over her mug.

"It's too early in the morning to be doing Mona Lisa imitations," Norman sighed. "I hope you know what you're doing."

So do I, Norman. So do I.

"Did you at least talk to him about the presentation to the committee?" he asked hopefully.

No, she hadn't, she thought guiltily. The time never seemed right to broach it. "The subject didn't come up."

"But the benefit will," he pointed out. "This *is* your baby, you know."

"I know, I know."

"Sorry," Norman said, retracting. "I keep forgetting that I'm not the big, bad producer anymore."

"You were never bad, Norman," she said fondly.

He winked. "Don't be too sure of that." The conversation shifted into a more relaxed tone. "So, what do you intend to do about Blankenship?"

"Where is he?" she asked, setting down her cup.

"Probably still in bed, getting his beauty sleep before the flight back."

Maggi became alarmed. "You booked him a flight to California?"

Norman shrugged. "He insisted. Said he'd sue for verbal breach of promise if I didn't." He sighed again, this time louder. "I told you, the man's unhappy. He wants to leave the show."

"But to book him a flight back now—"

"There wasn't anything else to do. He wouldn't even talk to me." Norman leaned over and patted her hand. "Besides, I knew the cavalry would be back today."

"Charge," Maggi mumbled, getting up. "Hold down the fort," she said over her shoulder. "And don't let any more of the soldiers leave."

"Watch out for the Indians," Norman advised as he braced himself to take his first sip of coffee.

Maggi found Blankenship waiting for her. Actually, what he was really waiting for was to have his ego stroked and soothed. It took half an hour of appealing and flattering, but Maggi managed not only to talk the choreographer into staying, but into cutting his opening number by three minutes. Maggi figured the audience could tolerate nine minutes of dancing movie stars early in the evening. Later, though the show had to move much quicker to keep the audience from getting restless. She went back to Norman to report her success.

Norman looked at her with unabashed admiration. "The UN delegation called. They'd like to have you join their team when this is over," he cracked. "Oh—" he stopped her as she reached the door "—Sommerfield called while you were out."

She perked up. "What did he say?"

"Nothing much to me." Norman answered with an innocent shrug. "Said he'd call back later." Maggi tried not to let her frustration show as she went back to her own office. Later, she thought.

But later found her busy elsewhere. She had promised the ticket buyers to deliver one hundred and fifty stars. The first seventy-five all decided to arrive Monday morning, at different times. When Maggi wasn't coordinating shuttles back and forth from the airport, she was going from room to room at the Ambassador, making sure that all of them had received the little complimentary perks that would make them feel their efforts were appreciated. Champagne, flowers, perfume, complimentary theater tickets, were all placed out in plain view for the visiting luminaries to see upon entering their respective rooms.

"But I've already seen this, dear," Donna Bradford dropped the tickets into Maggi's hand with a sniff when Maggi greeted her in her room. The popular actress's wide blue eyes told Maggi that she expected something done to rectify the situation immediately. "But I haven't seen *Native*," she purred. "Front-row seats?"

Native was sold out and would continue to be so for the next three months. Norman had already checked it out. But there was no use telling that to Donna, who was known to be laid low by mysterious "illnesses" when she wasn't happy.

"I'll see what I can do," Maggi promised.

"Make it three, Maggi dear. I ran into a couple of old friends on the flight."

"Three," Maggi repeated.

She moved heaven and earth and found a place for the theater manager's family during the taping of the benefit. The three tickets arrived by messenger at Donna's door later that afternoon.

And so it went. Some of the arrivals were gracious, some eager to join in the effort that Maggi was involved in, and some, like Donna, demanded to be pampered. Maggi felt her energies being sapped. During the production of the movies she had been involved with in the past six years, there had always been a temperamental star who needed placating, sometimes two. Now she was faced with an army of overgrown children, as Norman called them, to coddle and keep happy until the fittings, the rehearsals and the taping were over. It was a feat, Maggi thought, equal only to trying to teach a centipede how to tap-dance in syncopated rhythm.

Maggi wondered if she was going to make it.

She didn't connect with Brent the entire day. Each time he called, she was out and when she had the time to return his calls, she was informed in crisp, cool tones that "Mr. Sommerfield is in conference." The message sounded as if it pleased the soon-to-be-departed secretary no end.

TUESDAY WAS LIKE MONDAY, except played at 45 rpm instead of 33. Maggi had spent perhaps five hours in bed the previous night, and one of those hours was taken up by making last-minute notes on the first sketch they had decided to use. The director in charge had not yet arrived and Maggi was anxious for everything to be perfect.

Even then, in the midst of her exhaustion and the scribbled notes, she had been lonely. Her bed felt far too large for her, like a sweater that had suddenly been stretched out and now flopped shapelessly over her shoulders and wrists. She missed Brent. Having been with him a total of three days, she missed him.

Ah, but they hadn't been three ordinary days. They were blissful, wonderful days made up of sunshine and bits of starlight. She pushed aside some papers on her desk, closed her eyes and massaged her temples. Only Tuesday. Ten more days until the benefit. Ten more torturous days.

Ethel knocked and stopped singing "Summertime" long enough to tell Maggi that she was needed down at rehearsal.

"ALL RIGHT, ED," Maggi said, walking onstage. "I got your SOS. What's the problem?" She tried to sound cheerful, but it was getting difficult.

"I do magic, Cole." Blankenship draped an already sweat-soaked sweatshirt sleeve over her shoulder and led her aside. "I do not do miracles. Lauren Lang moves like a pregnant cow."

Although Maggi didn't care for the star who thought of herself as bigger than life, she thought the remark was a little unfair. "Nonsense, Ed—"

"Have you—" his voice cracked from the tension, and he lowered it, "—have you seen her dance?"

"No, but I wasn't referring to your judgment of her abilities," Maggi said in a low conspiratorial voice. "I was talking about you not being able to perform miracles. We both know better. I saw the Dane-Peters special. You made Dane and Esther Allen look like Fred and Ginger.''

''Yes, I did, didn't I?'' Blankenship smiled for a moment, content to bask in compliments and in the memory of that feat.

''Lauren's a lot more graceful-looking than Esther,'' Maggi prodded gently.

''Well . . .'' He scratched his jaw as he looked sideways at the sulking star who had been chosen as the centerpiece of the number. Maggi surmised that the casting director had probably thought the audience would be more interested in watching the voluptuous woman's body than her feet.

''You can do it,'' Maggi said encouragingly, and with that she left the stage.

''Lauren, darling, we're going to try it again. And this time, we'll try to stay conscious, won't we?''

Oh, well, Maggi shrugged. The man was never going to be voted Mr. Congeniality.

She walked to the back of the auditorium. Maggi's hand hovered over the doorknob, waiting to hear a squeal of indignant protest coming from Lauren.

It didn't come.

Maggi sighed with relief. Just then, the door swung open in front of her and she glanced up to see who was coming in. The one person she didn't expect to see was the one who was standing before her.

''Brent!''

''Ah, so you remember the name,'' he said dryly.

She gave him a quick, enthusiastic hug. "What are you doing here?"

"If Mohammad won't come to the mountain," he said expansively, leaning against the doorway, "or return the mountain's calls—"

Maggi's eyes grew wide. "I did too return the calls. The mountain's secretary is just being perverse."

"Speaking of whom, she's quitting."

Maggi looked surprised. She didn't think Marietta could have been dislodged with dynamite. "To what do you owe the happy occurrence?"

"You, I gather."

"Me?"

"Excuse me."

Brent and Maggi moved out of the way as two men carrying large pieces of equipment struggled through.

"Now this is more like it," Brent commented when the second man bumped into him, forcing him to move even closer to Maggi.

Their bodies were touching and Maggi couldn't help thinking how wonderful it felt to be close to him again. "How did I make her quit?"

"Seems Marietta has an aversion to clandestine affairs."

"Clandestine?" Maggi laughed. "Us?"

"Well, we could be if you'd return my call."

"I *did* return your call," she insisted.

"No matter, I'm here in the flesh. How about lunch, or have you eaten?"

"Maggi, can you come here, please?" a red-haired man in overalls called to her from the stage.

"Call this barbarian off, Cole. I'm working!" Blankenship ordered.

Maggi looked at Brent ruefully. "No, I haven't eaten, but there's no time right now. Listen, darling, if you have a moment, maybe you could wait?"

Brent hesitated. "Digby's circling the block. There's not a parking space to be had for miles."

"I know, I know," she said soothingly, unconsciously lapsing into the tone she had used all day. "This'll take just a minute."

But it didn't take just a minute. The set designer had thoughts that disagreed with actually constructing the set for the opening number. Blankenship had a few comments to add to the argument. By the time Maggi resolved that, there was another problem that needed her attention.

When she finally got back to where she had left Brent sitting, the seat was empty.

"What's the matter?" Norman asked, walking into the auditorium. He saw the unmasked look of disappointment on her face.

"Nothing," Maggi lied, holding her head for effect. "Just a little tired."

"I've got something to make you feel more tired," Norman apologized. "One of the creditors just called and insisted on talking to you."

She nodded. "I'll be right there."

"Oh, Maggi!" someone called from the stage. "Can I see you for a minute?"

HE WONDERED if it was a mistake. She seemed so wrapped up in what she was doing. If it had been any other profession in the world, he knew it wouldn't have bothered him—he understood dedication, respected it—but she was enmeshed in show business. The cutthroat business that had claimed his brother, that had claimed a lot of others, too. Show business had taken Jackie away from him, taken his time, his attention and, finally his very life. And now it was taking Maggi. He tried to tell himself that it was just for the duration of the benefit, but he knew that there would be other benefits, other shows, all competing with him for her time. Would he ultimately lose her, one way or another, because of it?

He couldn't control his resentfulness, nor look at the situation logically. All he had to go on was the past.

And what of their relationship? Was there a relationship? Or had he misread what was there in a moment of weakness, a moment of need? Was he seeing something that wasn't there? He was beginning to waver again. Was she only with him because of the financial backing she needed?

He wanted to think that she wasn't, but he honestly didn't know. Show business was the business of illusions, of making people believe in things that weren't real. Was Maggi merely casting an illusion? He didn't know if he could take devastating disappointment twice in his life.

It began to rain. A steady beat of drops hit against his window. Lost in thought, he watched the rivulets of water merge into one another.

"I'M SORRY," Maggi said finally getting Brent on the phone. It had taken over forty-five minutes to do it. Turned away by Marietta twice, in desperation Maggi finally put Ethel on the job. She promised her a position in the huge finale lineup. All she had to do was get past Marietta.

Necessity wasn't the mother of invention, desperation was, Maggi thought as Ethel triumphantly transferred the call to her. Renée, the makeup artist, could be called on to transform Ethel into a swan. As long as the swan didn't try to sing, they'd be all right.

"I understand," Brent said.

His voice was cool. "No, you don't, but I wasn't fair to you either. I'd like a chance to make amends."

His reserve began to melt. "What kind of a chance?"

"Any sort you'd like."

"Dinner?"

"Oh, Brent, I—" She stopped herself before forming the word "can't" *You'll lose him. Remember what he thinks of your world.* "Late?" she asked hopefully.

"How late?"

"Ten?"

"I'll see if I can hold out."

"And, um, Brent?"

"Yes?"

"We're going to have to talk about—about my seeing the committee."

His hand involuntarily tightened on the receiver even while he told himself that it wasn't the way it sounded. She wasn't just calling him about that. After all, it was the need for backing that had originally brought her to him.

And kept her with him?

"Yes, Maggi," he promised. "We'll talk."

Maggi had a very unsettled feeling as she hung up the phone. She knew that the benefit was a bone of contention between them, but she had to make him aware that there was a lot of good coming out of the entertainment world, that it wasn't all bad. It was a hard feat to do when all he saw were the demands, the egos, the tempers. Norman had been trying to line up another foundation, but so far he was having no luck. Funds seemed to be tight everywhere. The Wallaby Foundation was their only hope. *If* she could get to talk to the committee. Why was Brent stalling? Was it really because the committee wasn't convening until Monday? Wasn't it in his power to grant her the funds if the committee was unavailable? Her head began to ache.

"Damn!" she muttered.

"Ms. Cole?" Ethel stood in the doorway, hesitantly.

"Yes?" She wondered if this headache would leave by the time the taping was over.

"Um, about my part?"

She had never seen such raw hope flaring in a person's entire countenance before. Maggi rose with a smile. "C'mon," she said, putting her arm around the young woman's shoulders. "Let's see how we can fit you in."

If anyone could fit her in, it would be Blankenship. If he didn't eat her alive first.

The phone shrilled. "Norman, answer that, please," Maggi called over her shoulder as she passed his door.

The phone went on ringing.

Chapter Twelve

"I trust everything is satisfactory," Saunders said. The grandfather clock in the foyer had just chimed eleven. He made it plain that he wasn't used to serving dinner at such an ungodly hour. Saunders leveled his stare at Maggi. "Unless, of course, Madam has some vendetta against chicken."

Maggi presented him with her best smile. Despite his caustic wit, she liked Saunders. He reminded her of the stereotype, droll butler who could always be found in those wonderful comedies from the thirties she loved so much. "Madam has no score to settle with chicken, thank you, Saunders. I'm sure everything is perfect."

"Of course it is," the man said as he withdrew.

"Is it?" Brent asked after a moment.

"Hmm?" Maggi was savoring her first bite of chicken Kiev. She suddenly felt as if she hadn't eaten in weeks. Nibbling on sandwiches while dashing in and out of hotel rooms and her office couldn't really be considered eating; it was barely surviving. For the life of her, she couldn't remember what she had eaten for lunch, except that it had left an aftertaste.

"Are things perfect?"

Maggi bit her lip and raised her eyes. He was staring at her intently. Something was wrong again. *What's he getting at? He's not the type to hunt for a compliment.* "They are right now."

How was he going to word this? "Maggi, do you enjoy all that, all that—"

"Commotion?" she suggested helpfully.

"I was thinking of madness, actually."

"Yes, that, too." She paused for a moment to take a sip of wine. She was stalling. She needed time to think. *Careful. He's got a funny look in his eyes.*

Oh, what the hell; he deserves the truth.

But can he take it? And can you take his reaction to it if he doesn't like it?

Truth won.

"While I'm in the middle of it all, I think that I must be utterly crazy to get involved in the hundred and one details that go into making a good production. And this—this is the biggest thing I've ever tried. But I have to admit that no matter how exhausting work can sometimes be, by the time I'm two weeks into a vacation, I get, well, itchy."

"Itchy?"

She nodded. "I can't wait to get back into the fray. I know it sounds crazy, but I love it." She looked at him hopefully. *Please try to understand.*

Brent grew very silent. He was trying to reconcile Maggi's feelings with his own. For the time being, he felt that it was best to say nothing.

Maggi could feel the silence encroaching on them. For the first time in days, silence between them made her uncomfortable. It carried with it a terrible uncertainty. She couldn't put her finger on it. She felt like a blindfolded fighter lashing out at an opponent she wasn't allowed to see.

Did he still bear animosity toward her? Against her world? She had to say something to try to bring it out in the open and resolve their differences once and for all. This was so frustrating. After the wonderful time they had had, there still seemed to be some unsettled problems.

When they had finished eating their meal, he led her out to the terrace. The cool night air made her shiver, and he put his arm around her shoulder. They were all alone in the world. Alone with the bells of St. Patrick's Cathedral below them—St. Patrick's, candles. Thoughts linked together in Maggi's mind in a kaleidoscopic manner. *Talk to him now.*

"The seven years I spent away from the studios were seven years in limbo." She felt the arm about her shoulders tighten slightly, as if Brent were bracing himself against an invisible foe. She drew on her reserve courage and went on. He had to see that everything associated with Hollywood wasn't terrible. "I grew up, went to school, got married, all the while feeling as if I were living on the outside, looking in."

"The outside," he said slowly, turning the words around as if examining them.

"Yes, the outside." She avoided the dark look she saw in his eyes by looking up at the stars overhead. "I grew up in Hollywood. I didn't just break in at eight. My bottom showed up in diaper commercials. I lisped in admiration over how clean my mother's sheets were when she used the right detergent," Maggi grinned. "And I was in enough breakfast commercials to sour me on cereal for the rest of my life."

"I have to make a note to Saunders not to serve you corn flakes," Brent said wryly, taking a long drink from his glass.

"I was lucky enough to come in at the tail end of the child star boom. Life, as you know, was peaches and cream for a while, a very short while, but it got me hooked."

"How hooked?"

She couldn't read the emotion behind his words. *Just tell him everything and be done with it.* "Hooked enough to want always to be around the stardust. That's what drew me back to Norman in the first place."

"I can't imagine anyone being drawn back to Norman." Brent moved to the table to pour himself another glass of wine. He raised an inquisitive eyebrow in Maggi's direction. Maggi stepped back to pass him her half-empty glass, then leaned over the railing and looked down into the dark night.

"Oh, don't let Norman put you off. He's a little like Saunders."

"Saunders?" Brent echoed in surprise. "I really don't see how—"

She turned back to him. He handed her her glass. "Protective of territorial rights."

He took his place beside her. "And what territorial rights does Norman have?" he asked gamely.

"He gave me my start in production. He was my director on several pictures before that and he was the closest thing I ever had to a father." She took a deep sip. "Oh, yes," she said in answer to the surprised look on Brent's face. "You weren't the only one who grew up without a father around. Mine left before I took my first step. Something about not being able to cope with the responsibility of being a father. Great burden, that," she said, pushing back the memory as she cradled the drink between the palms of her hands. "For years I felt I had to make it up to my mother that my father left because of me. Maybe that's what drove me so hard." She looked down into her glass, not seeing it at all. "I'm talking too much. You'd think I'd be all talked out by now. I've been doing it all day."

"Then stop," he suggested. He put down his glass and took hers from her hands. He took her into his arms, his heart going out to the helpless little waif that existed within the woman.

She never did manage to broach the subject of the foundation's support that night.

"YES, YES, THAT'S FINE," Maggi said, giving her approval to the press releases that one of her assistants showed her. She smiled at the one in her hand. "Big-

gest Blockbuster of All Time'' the bold black letters
proclaimed. Until the next one, she mused. There was
always a biggest show, to be trounced by another,
bigger, more extravagant one. Well, she wasn't going
for extravagance, she was going for the money. That
home and hospital needed to be renovated. There was
always something breaking down, going wrong, beg-
ging for repairs, and who could recover in a place that
was in worse shape than its patients? No, this was her
cause, her way of paying back for the wonderful
memories of her youth and for the lucrative last ten
years spent on the opposite side of the camera.

The opposite side of the camera.

The phrase echoed in her brain and lingered as she
watched Harold Cunningham, the director, rehearse
a sketch. What quirk of fate had put her on the side of
the ugly ducklings at age thirteen? What would her life
be like right now if she had been able to make the
transition from lollipops to roses with the ease that
Elizabeth Taylor had? Or Roddy McDowall? Neither
of them had been plagued by hands and feet that suddenly mushroomed ahead of other body parts. Neither of them had transformed when they had hit
thirteen into something that only their mothers could
love.

She sighed. Her adolescence had been horrid. She
had gone through all the motions she had told Brent
about last night, but her soul had yearned to be back
in front of the camera no matter what she had told
Norman and her mother to the contrary. What would
it have been like?

Hold it. Let's not get carried away here. You're the producer, not the star. You have more clout, more staying power than almost any of these people flying in for your show. You, at least, know where your next meal is coming from.

Very sensible words. But at that particular moment they didn't help. Perhaps it was all the old faces that she had seen that day. She had insisted on a "stars of yesteryear" segment and had been rewarded with a shower of telegrams and calls from many past luminaries who were eager to show up for a moment in the limelight. She had worked with many of them. Nostalgia hung heavy in the air and about her soul.

"You look as if you're miles away, Maggi. Anything wrong with the prince?"

Maggi realized that Norman was standing next to her in the wings. How long had he been there, watching her? "No, as a matter of fact, the prince is coming to see a rehearsal today. I thought it might be good for him to watch."

Norman looked unconvinced. "Whatever you say." He paused to catch a punch line and chuckled. "You know, that sounds a lot funnier than it reads."

Maggi nodded absently. "Norman," she began tentatively.

He had known her long enough to recognize the tone. Something was on her mind. "Yes?"

"Do you think that I could have made it?" She turned to look at him. He saw the uncertain look in her eyes. "I mean, if I had gotten involved later, do you think that I could have—"

Norman kissed her on the cheek. "You would have knocked them all on their ear, Maggi. But you had brains. You elected to stay on this side of the fence."

"Wasn't much of an election. The ballot box was stuffed ahead of time."

"Lucky you. Oh-oh, I believe you've just had a special delivery." Norman leaned out as he squinted his eyes to make out the figure walking down the center aisle. "The man of the hour has arrived."

"Where?" Maggi asked, pushing past Norman's protruding stomach.

"That's it, play hard to get, Maggi," he commented, stepping back. "Oh, McNalley wants you to call him back as soon as possible."

"McNalley," she sighed. The man at the airlines who was in charge of securing the tickets for them, the man she had promised to pay back as soon as she was able—except that the funds were being stretched to the limit as it was.

"I'm very sorry, Mrs. Cole," the falsetto voice had said on the phone the last time they had talked. She doubted McNalley was sorry at all. "But I simply must insist on the final payment. I do have my responsibility to the company, you do understand."

What she understood was that the pressure was mounting. All those stars couldn't be asked to pay their own way. They expected tickets, first-class tickets. If one flew first class, they all flew first class. There could be no preferential treatment.

Maggi nodded. "I'll call him first chance I get," she promised Norman, hoping that her first chance would be after the show was over. At the moment, the actual show was her biggest headache. All the airplane tickets had been mailed out. She'd have to worry about paying for them some other time.

"This'd be a good time to put the question to your boyfriend," were Norman's departing words.

But was it? Was it really a good time? *Stop wavering like a giddy schoolgirl. This is important. You're not asking him for yourself, you're asking for everyone.*

So why isn't everyone else suddenly experiencing the butterflies she felt in her stomach?

"You came," Maggi said happily, linking her arm with his.

"I had to postpone a meeting, but I came."

"Not with the committee?" she asked.

He caught the tone of her voice. "No, not with the committee. They won't be convening until the beginning of next week."

"Next week," she echoed unhappily.

"I told you, Maggi—"

"These things can't be rushed," she chimed in with him. "I'm sorry, it's just that I'm being pressured to come up with the money."

She made a pretty picture, even pleading for money, and that was what he surmised she was doing, in a fashion. Those big, lustrous eyes could probably get a donation from a Bowery bum. But then, a Bowery bum wouldn't have to worry about losing her to an intangible force.

He almost hadn't come today. He had almost reached for the phone to tell her that he had urgent business elsewhere. He really didn't want to see her in this element, didn't want to see how much a part of it she was. It made her that much less a part of him.

"Sit," Maggi gestured to the front row. "I want you to watch this. It's a little rough, but I think you might get a kick out of it." *I hope you get a kick out of it*.

They sat through the first production number. To Blankenship's credit, he had performed magic. Twenty-five stars, with left-footed Lauren Lang at the center, performed more than admirably well, even though most of them were out of their element.

Maggi stifled an urge to jump up on the stage and kiss Blankenship. The show was going to be all right!

"Um, Maggi," the director called as the dancers all melted backstage, "we need a stand-in for Candace Parton."

Candace had promised to come with the first wave of stars, but in typical fashion, she had called to say that she had to fly in at a later date.

"Well, I—"

"How about you?" George Garfield's voice boomed out, filling the dark auditorium. Once a star of high caliber, he lived now in semiretirement, making more money doing commercial voice-overs for coffee and cars than he ever had in his heyday.

She smiled and began to demur. She leaned toward Brent. "George Garfield played my father in *Bringing up Julia*. I guess that entitles him to order me around."

She was grinning from ear to ear, Brent thought. She was remembering what it was like and missing it. He had seen Jackie do enough reminiscing to understand the longing look. She still missed it.

"Oh, how about it, Maggi? Help us out. It's just for today," Cunningham urged, waving a script at her.

"Well, I . . . okay. Why not? It'll be fun." She gave Brent a quick kiss on the lips. "I'll be right back," she promised. "It's a short piece."

She ran up the side steps to the stage with more zest to her step than she had felt all day.

"I'm going to be really terrible at this," she warned Cunningham, taking the script.

"George here told me otherwise." The director scratched his thinning red hair. "I never knew you were in pictures."

"A million years ago," Maggi said with a wave of her hand.

George Garfield cleared his throat deliberately.

"Sorry, George, *half* a million years ago." Her eyes were shining merrily.

Brent could almost swear he saw them gleam from where he sat. She was excited about this. There was a different zest to her now from what there had been when he dropped by yesterday. Yesterday, she had been happy but harried. Today, onstage, it was as if a cup of water had just been offered her after a drought.

She looked too enthusiastic, too happy. It was in her blood. She was an actress.

Brent watched in silence, listening to her read while blocking out the others. Even at the first run-through, she was letter-perfect. Her timing was faultless. The skit ended with a few bars from a duet with the elderly Garfield. She had a pleasing voice that rose and swelled above Garfield's. Brent frowned. She was a natural. His doubts grew. *Was* she merely acting when she was with him? Was he being duped by an expert?

And if not, would the industry always be his permanent rival?

He felt left out of her world, didn't like it to begin with. Was that her first love? Would it draw her away from him time and again? He felt a surge of jealousy and tried vainly to control it.

Applause filled the air as the people backstage showed their approval. Maggi beamed and blushed.

"Hey, that was wonderful," Cunningham was genuinely pleased. He began to look at Maggi in a new light. "Listen, if for some reason Candace doesn't show—"

"She'll show," Maggi said, pushing the manuscript back into the director's hands.

He wouldn't take it. "But if she doesn't, will you take the part?"

"The show must go on, Maggi," Garfield said, peering around Cunningham's thin frame. "Hey, I've got an idea." He put one paw on the director's shoulder. "Why don't we do a duet from *Bringing Up Julia*?" he suggested. "Do you remember that number we sang, somewhere in the middle? It was about—"

"No, I'm sorry, George," she said kindly. "I've retired from all that."

"With that voice, you shouldn't have," Cunningham told her, looking down at his notes to see what the next number was to be. "Keep the script, just in case." He winked.

She pressed the pages to her chest. "Thank you, gentlemen, you've made my day," she said graciously. "But I've someone waiting for me." With that, she extricated herself from the stage and bounded down the stairs.

"Know what?" she said, dropping into the seat next to Brent, her voice breathless.

"You enjoyed yourself," Brent finished for her.

"Did it show?"

"All over your face. You were good, very good."

She sat up and turned to look at him. "Did you really think so?" She was being silly, she knew, but she longed for his approval, his above all the others.

"I wouldn't have said it if I didn't mean it," he told her, trying to keep his thoughts from showing. It was ridiculous for a man of thirty-nine to be jealous of an inanimate thing, but he was. He was jealous of the excitement this all brought to her, jealous of the claim it had on her affections.

Maggi sensed his shift in mood. "C'mon," she said, taking his hand, "before they tap me to help on set construction. Someone may have found out I once built a birdhouse."

She led him out of the auditorium and up the stairs to her office.

"This is what I really wanted you to see," Trying to clear a spot on her cluttered desk, she unfurled a large drawing. "Doesn't look like very much on paper, I suppose, but these are the renovation plans for the retirement home. There's going to be a little theater workshop here and a stage with an area for lighting and an orchestra over here." She tapped a place on the plans. "No, oops, I've just put the orchestra in the duck pond."

"Duck pond?" He looked down for the first time.

"Well, now that I've got your attention, want to tell me what's bothering you?" she said, rolling up the blueprints again. She snapped the rubber band in place.

"Nothing."

I don't believe you. "Good, because that's as it should be. There shouldn't be anything wrong between us." Maggi dropped the blueprints on her desk and passed her arms through his, wrapping them about his waist. "I know that I must seem pretty preoccupied to you right now, but it's all for a good cause, I swear it is. After I finish this, I have no obligations for a month. We can spend some time together then—if you're still interested."

"What do you mean 'still'?"

She let go of him. "Well, I dunno," she said in a Freddie Freeloader accent, "some people don't care to hang around with, y'know, has-beens." For emphasis, she kicked at imaginary dust.

"I wish," Brent said, putting his arms round her and pulling her close to him, dangerously close, "that you were a 'never-was.'"

"Oh, don't say that," she said playfully, reverting to her own voice. "If I were a florist somewhere in Carpinteria, California, I would never have had a reason to scale the walls of your private citadel and we wouldn't be standing in my office on the verge of a deep, meaningful kiss."

The tense lines in his face relaxed, much to her relief. "Well, we're standing in your office all right, but where's the deep, meaningful kiss?"

"I thought you'd never ask." Maggi raised herself on her toes.

Two lines on the phone began to ring at once. She ignored them as her lips met Brent's. Her intercom buzzed, joining the din.

Brent's mouth left hers, but he had a tolerant smile on his lips. "I'm almost used to hearing bells when I kiss you, but buzzers are something new."

"My intercom," she said lamely.

"You'd better answer it before your secretary breaks a finger pushing on it."

Maggi depressed her switch. "Yes, Ethel?"

"That man from the airline is on line two again.

Maggi took a deep breath, then made a decision. "Tell him I'm still out. And, Ethel, hold all the other calls."

"But—"

Maggi let go of the intercom buzzer. "You were saying?"

The smile he gave her went straight to her heart. "As I recall, I wasn't saying anything. I was kissing a woman who had just made her triumphant comeback to the stage.''

"I was never on the stage."

"Her triumphant debut, then."

She laughed when he said it, but she couldn't rid herself of an underlying concern. Just how much did all this still bother him?

"Well, then, get on with what you were doing," she urged, "before we're interrupted again. I need an energy boost."

"Always glad to do my bit," he said, lowering his mouth to hers.

Maggi sighed as his lips touched hers. This was what she had been longing for all day, thinking about it in the back of her mind. Once again, she both damned and blessed the cause that had brought them together. How was she ever going to get him to see things her way?

If only someone would write her a happy ending, she thought, losing herself in his kiss.

Chapter Thirteen

Maggi's peaceful interlude didn't last long. Ethel appeared in her doorway, hesitantly peering in. She knocked once, faintly.

Maggi saw the woman out of the corner of her eye. Reluctantly, her arms dropped from about Brent. "What is it, Ethel?"

Ethel looked embarrassed for having been caught staring. "I—I just came in to tell you that your daughter is on the line."

"Which one?" Maggi looked at the two bright lights on her phone.

There was a long pause. "Nikki, I think she said."

Maggi laughed. "No, I meant which line."

"Three."

"Thank you, Ethel." A soft smile touched Maggi's lips as she picked up the phone. "Nikki?"

"Hi, Mom, where are you?" Nikki asked cheerfully.

"Right here," Maggi answered, puzzled.

"And we're right here," Nikki told her. Maggi could hear the tolerant grin in her voice.

"Right— Oh, my God, it's Thursday!"

"Yes, it is."

Maggi groaned. "It's Thursday," she muttered to Brent.

"Is that a problem?" he asked. He hadn't a clue as to what was going on.

"I missed the girls' flight," Maggi explained. "I'll be right over to pick you up," she promised Nikki, reaching for the drawer with her purse.

"It's okay, Mom, we can take a cab to the hotel. Just be there, okay? Love you."

"I love you too, Nikki," Maggi said, hanging up. She sank down on the sofa both tired and agitated. "I forgot to pick them up at the airport," she told Brent ruefully. "I've been so busy welcoming movie stars, television stars and recording artists that I neglected to meet my own daughters."

If she could forget about her own daughters, girls she beamed over every time she mentioned them to him, where did that put him in the scheme of things? The industry was a mighty opponent, he thought.

Brent sat down next to her. "Maybe all this is too much for you?" he said hopefully.

Maggi missed his meaning. "No, I'm just a little overwhelmed at the moment." She sat up straighter and turned to him. "Would you like to come to dinner tonight and meet them? They're really terrific kids."

"They had a terrific example to follow." He leaned over and kissed her fondly. Despite the kiss, Maggi detected a note of sadness in his voice. She tried to erase it with a warm smile. "Is that yes or no?"

"That's a definite yes. Tell me, is there any way I can entice you away from all this?" He nodded at the littered desk and the brightly lit phone.

"I'm really sorry, Brent." Her playful mood faded. She glanced at her watch as the phone began to ring again. "I've got half a million things to take care of before tonight."

"I take it that's my cue," he said, rising.

Maggi followed suit. She took hold of Brent's lapels as she raised herself on her toes. She kissed him soundly. "That's what I like about you, you're so understanding."

But he wasn't, he thought as he left. He wasn't understanding at all. He was battling the dogs of jealousy, and he was losing ground.

MAGGI'S DAUGHTERS looked like theme and variations of their mother, Brent thought when he met them. Both girls had their mother's fair complexion, her high cheekbones, her green eyes and her slight build. And they had her hair. Nikki, older by eleven months, wore hers in a short cut, barely coming down to her ears. Rachel wore hers down to her waist, a long river of copper. Looking at them over dinner, Brent couldn't believe that Maggi had ever had an "ugly" stage. None of the three women at the table looked as if she had known a plain moment in her life.

Maggi watched Brent as she ate and kept up a steady stream of conversation. She was worried about Brent's reaction to the girls and more specifically, to her having a family.

You're thinking "permanent," Maggi. There's no reason you should be doing that. This is just an interlude, nothing more.

But her mind couldn't get her heart to believe that.

"I'm really not going to have too much time for you, I'm afraid," Maggi apologized.

"We're used to that," Rachel answered without a trace of resentment. "We've learned that it's quality, not quantity, where Mom's concerned," she explained to Brent.

"Besides, there are so many fringe benefits to having Mom in the business," Nikki chimed in. "How many other girls can say that they had Robert Redford at their sweet sixteen party?"

"That was her one wish," Maggi explained. "Nikki keeps her requests down to a minimum," she added wryly.

"How long are you staying in New York?" Brent asked.

"Until the show is over," Nikki answered. Of the two, she was the more talkative. Rachel preferred to watch and listen. "We're here on spring vacation." She winked. "And a little extra.

"What did you do with Ada?" Maggi suddenly realized that her housekeeper hadn't accompanied the girls. God, she was getting bad. She should have been at the airport. Maybe this *was* getting to be too much for her, after all.

"Mom, we're old enough to be traveling without a chaperone." Nikki turned to Brent. "Don't you think that at sixteen and seventeen, we're old enough to travel alone?"

"Definitely" Brent smiled.

"I like him, Mom, he's sensible," Nikki said.

Maggi wondered if she could slide under the table without being missed. But rather than look annoyed at Nikki's very blatant attempt at matchmaking, Brent only laughed.

"I was essentially on my own at sixteen, so I'm the last person to say that's too young." He covered Maggi's hand with his own, marveling at how easily gestures like that now came to him. He couldn't recall ever having been demonstrative.

Nikki looked at Brent and rose rather abruptly. "Well, we've had a long flight, Mom, and I think we'd better turn in for the night. Let's go, Rach." She hustled her sister away from the last of her cherry pie.

"But I haven't finished yet," Rachel protested.

Nikki took the fork out of her hands. "That stuff goes directly to your hips, Rach," she warned. "Good night, Mom. Mr. Sommerfield." Both kissed their mother and were gone.

Maggi sat ruefully looking at Brent. "Rather obvious, weren't they?" she said with an embarrassed grin.

"A little eager, maybe. But no more than I," he said, walking around the table and taking her hand. "Where can we go to be alone?"

Maggi looked in the direction the girls had taken. Brent took the opportunity to kiss her neck lightly. Desire immediately invaded her body. She had absolutely no resistance to the man. But tonight she had to try. Tonight she was a mother. "Brent, the girls are here."

"I know," he murmured, kissing her again. The familiar liquid fire began to fill her. "I just met them remember?"

"But I just can't—"

"They're Hollywood children. Surely—"

Maggi put her hands on his shoulders and pushed him back. The look in her eyes was very, very serious. "No, not surely," she said to him firmly. "Never."

"Never?"

"Not since Johnny, my husband."

He believed her. It made him that much more grateful for what he had and that much more afraid at the same time. She was too attractive a woman not to have a legion of men at her beck and call except by choice. Did her choice mean that she was forever wedded to her work? To a world he had detested for so long?

He took her hands into his and brought them to his lips, kissing one at a time. "Maybe I had better go."

She felt an immediate pang. "Will I see you tomorrow?" *That's it, Maggi, play hard to get.* Norman's words rang in her head, but she didn't care. She wasn't good at games, not where her feelings were concerned. Games cluttered up the issue. And Brent was very, very important to her.

"Wild horses couldn't keep me away." He kissed her hands again. "Tomorrow night, we'll go to my place. Alone."

"You don't like the girls?" she asked.

"I like the girls just fine. But I like their mother more."

Like. He said like, not love. He's not the type to proclaim love, Maggi. Give the man time.

But she didn't need time. She was in love, hopelessly in love for the first time since Johnny. Maybe, she thought, for the first time ever.

FRIDAY PASSED like sap from a tree in mid-January. She felt like a prisoner marking time until parole. But she had to put her desire on hold. There were more snags to untangle. The hotel had booked both a hardrock star and a fading movie queen in the same room and neither one wanted to give up territorial rights once her baggage had been brought in.

"I don't know how this happened." The desk clerk apologized to Maggi as the two women regarded each other with obvious comtempt. "I can have another room ready immediately.

"Fine," the rock star said, jerking a thumb at the movie queen's luggage. "Get her junk out of here."

"I have no intention of leaving," Elizabeth Harrington said in the accented tones that had made her voice so distinctive in the fifties. "Maggi?" She looked expectantly at Maggi.

Yul Brynner wasn't the only one who got to play Solomon. Maggi weighed her options. The lady or the tiger? she thought, getting very weary of all the clashes of ego and temperament she had had to endure over the past few days and nights.

"You don't expect me to move my gear for her, do you?" Flavia asked with a toss of her multi-colored hair.

"Actually," Maggi began slowly, "I'm afraid I expect you both to move. The hotel has also booked this room for Sir John Alexander and I wouldn't want to make the poor man move." The name was enough to make Elizabeth retreat instantly. The going was slower with Flavia, who appeared unimpressed by one of the pillars of the movie industry. Maggi tried another ploy. "He's in his eighties and in failing health. Upsetting him might be, well, you know..." She let her voice trail off.

The appeal to her better nature worked, and Flavia withdrew her claim to the room.

The desk clerk sighed, muttering a host of apologies to Maggi as they left the room. "This has never happened before," he swore, lowering his voice. "But, Ms. Cole, I think you made a mistake. Sir Alexander is on the third floor."

"Yes, I know."

Mentally, he doffed his hat to Maggi as he left the battlefield to make proper arrangements.

THE CALL TO ATTEND REHEARSAL was the highlight of Maggi's afternoon. It was only a small five-minute skit, but she felt more alive while she was doing it than she had all day. The world of pretend had its rewards, she thought as she walked off the stage.

Her daughters, sitting with Norman, were in the tiny audience that watched her.

"Mom, you were great," Nikki said enthusiastically. "I didn't know you could really sing."

"I sang to you girls all the time when you were little," Maggi protested.

"Yeah, but that's different. Little kids always think their mothers can sing," Nikki said. "But you can *really* sing." She appeared very taken with the fact.

"I thought you were very good, Mom," Rachel added.

Maggi hugged her. "Thank you baby." She grinned at Nikki. "Thank you both." She turned to Norman. "So, are you going to take care of my girls this afternoon?"

"I was going to try, but they're just as stubborn as you are. They want to go off on their own."

Maggi looked doubtfully at her daughters.

"Just shopping, Mom," Nikki said. "I've always wanted to spend hours shopping in Macy's."

"And Bloomingdale's," Rachel added.

"I can see where Norman might get bored." Maggi laughed.

"Right about now," Norman said, "I could stand being bored with two beautiful ladies who didn't have demands."

"Oh, but we do." Nikki winked. "There's this dance coming up in May and I need—"

Maggi nodded, knowing the familiar routine. "Just don't go overboard. If I don't get the backing I need for this, your mother might be washing dishes at some backwater café after next Friday."

"Never happen," Nikki said, kissing her mother as she and Rachel began to take their leave. "You always find a way to come through. See you later."

"Six. Be back by six," Maggi called after them.

"They're big girls now."

"I keep forgetting," Maggi answered, then looked back at Norman. "Why is it that you tell me they're big girls and as far as I'm concerned, you keep telling me I have to be protected?"

"It isn't nice to point out your elders' contradictions, Maggi," he reproached her. "I just got a look at the meal tab at the hotel," he said, changing the subject abruptly. "Our stars have arrived hungry."

Maggi nodded, sliding down in her seat for a moment until her head rested against the back. She closed her eyes. She knew what was coming next.

"Any closer to—?"

"He said the committee is meeting on Monday."

"Five days, Maggi."

"I know, I know, we're cutting it close. But what other options do we have? All the other foundations that even remotely handle our kind of charity benefit have either already donated to our cause or can't." She sat up. "Norman, find out how many of our illustrious creditors can be stalled. I'm meeting with the representative from the cable station today. Maybe I can get him to come through with more money up front. In the meantime, talk to the creditors for me. Promise them anything. Your firstborn, anything."

"I'm not giving my dog," Norman told her. He considered the situation. "Maybe they'll take my ex-wife as collateral."

"You probably already tried that," she said laughing.

"Yeah, nobody wanted her." He paused for a moment before leaving her. "I thought you were good up there."

Her eyes lit up for a moment. "Did you?"

"You've got a funny look in your eyes, Maggi. You're not thinking of—"

"You know, Norman, there's something very addictive about applause. Once it gets in your blood, it's hard to shake it. You spend the rest of your life looking for it, expecting it, hoping for it."

"Hey, Maggi." Norman sat down again, alarmed. "Isn't a show and a man enough for you?"

"Well, I just—"

"Don't, don't tell me you want to get back up there in front of the lights."

"I might," she said. "But I doubt—"

"How long have you had this suicide complex?" he demanded. "It's not enough for you to be involved with a man who until two weeks ago wanted to have your head served on a platter? It's not enough that you're handling the biggest extravaganza since Noah tried to toilet train the animals on the ark? Now you're talking about going back into acting and all that trauma. Why not just take up skydiving and leave your chute on the plane?"

"Norman, you have such a colorful way of saying things." She gave him a soothing kiss. "I'm not talking about getting back into it," she lied. "I'm just saying that it really felt good up there, that's all."

That wasn't all and they both knew it. There was nothing for Norman to do but let the subject drop. "I'll see what I can do about the creditors," he said, shaking his head as he left.

"Thank you, Norman. I'll be back up in a few minutes. I just want to catch this comedy routine."

But it wasn't the comedy routine she really wanted to catch. It was her breath and her senses. Everything was happening at once. Everywhere she turned, there were demands on her and she didn't have a moment to herself. She both needed and wanted time alone with Brent. And because of it all, she had forgotten about her girls. Thank God they had grown up so level-headed and sensible.

And what of their mother? Had she grown up levelheaded and sensible? Was she being sensible? She had lied to Norman and she could tell he knew it. Part of her missed this, missed all of it terribly. She hadn't realized how much until she walked onto the stage. It was as if a floodgate had opened. She had almost agreed to do that old routine from *Bringing Up Julia* when George Garfield suggested it yesterday. She realized at that moment that there was still a hunger in her, a hunger she had thought was long burried.

As if you need that to add to your list of problems. If Brent only knew what was going on in your head...

"Brent." She said the name aloud, but the noise level was too high for anyone to hear her. She accepted the reason he had given her for not having gone to the board yet, but when she was away from him, she couldn't help wondering if perhaps, just perhaps, she was wrong about that. He stirred a fever in her blood the way no one else ever had, ever would. She was certain of that. But was she allowing all that to make her a victim of duplicity? Could he be setting her up for a trap after all?

She was putting all her marbles in one bag. If the foundation didn't come through with the donation, she was in really bad trouble unless she could find someone else to underwrite the balance of the bills. There wasn't anyone else to turn to, she reminded herself. She and Norman had exhausted all the possible avenues before they approached the Wallaby Foundation. Their only other recourse would be to take the needed money from the funds raised by the benefit. But that would leave them short of their goal. Maggi sighed.

Was Brent ultimately using her against herself, paying back not only her but Hollywood in general? What better revenge? Two with one blow.

The thought brought a shiver to her, a painful shiver. No, he couldn't be like that; he just couldn't be. He couldn't be hard-hearted enough not only to ruin her reputation but to lay low the hopes of so many people.

Actors, she reminded herself. And he had no use for actors. She had seen the way he looked when he spoke about his brother. He loved Jackie, and the industry had killed him as far as Brent was concerned. She knew he had relented, changed over the past few weeks, but she couldn't help being concerned. Would the old hatred crop up? Could it still destroy them all?

You're just overtired, Maggi. You're trying to do too many things at once and you're feeling guilty over not being super-everything, that's all.

But she wasn't sure if that was all, and it ate at her.

Chapter Fourteen

Brent sat in his office, lost in thought. It took a moment for the sound of the intercom to register with him. He was in no mood for business, he thought impatiently. Of late, he had been too preoccupied to think clearly. She had done that to him. She had brought disorder into his well-organized world. But she had also brought rainbows, a whole pocketful of rainbows. He was feeling things, finally feeling things after such a long time. He had thought that he was devoid of feelings, but she had proven him wrong.

The buzzer sounded again.

"Yes?"

"Mr. Wainwright to see you, sir." The soft, Southern lilt over the intercom was pleasing. Marietta had decided to take an "opportunity elsewhere," as she had stated so tersely. She hadn't even given the customary two-week notice. Diane was a pleasant substitute, competent and quiet. Her opinions, if she had any, were not expressed on her face as Marietta's had been.

"Shall I send him in?" Diane asked hesitantly when there was no answer.

What is wrong with me? "Yes, of course."

Walter Wainwright was his second in command. The man was ten years older than Brent and looked twenty years older. But he never resented the fact that Brent had been put over him. He never stood, waiting in the shadows, hoping for a misstep the way so many of the others did. Brent smiled to himself. Maybe there was a little bit of Hollywood in every business. But not in Wainwright. The man was jovial, as outgoing as Brent was reserved. Together, they complemented one another.

"What can I do for you, Walter?" Brent asked as the heavyset man walked in.

"I've just had a chance to look at this Maggi Cole application," Walter said, taking a seat without waiting to be asked. "Wasn't she that little girl in all those musicals?"

Trust Walter to remember that. Walter was a trivia buff, a movie aficionado. He was the only one on the committee, probably the only one in the foundation, who knew about Brent's connection to Jackie. He had guessed it after looking into Brent's records. Walter had been trying to drag him to a movie for years now, insisting that he needed to unwind, to relax. Wouldn't Walter be surprised to find out just how relaxed he had become in the company of a former movie star?

"Yes, she was. Maggi McCree."

"Maggie McCree." The name seemed to take him back. "Wonderful how she bounced back, don't you think?"

"Bounced back?"

"Made a new career for herself," Walter clarified, feeling around his jacket pockets for a match. His pipe lay dormant, unlit in his left hand. "Well, what do you think about the application?" he asked, leaning forward. "What's your recommendation?"

Brent paused for a moment, gathering his thoughts together. Walter's question echoed in his mind. "Wonderful how she bounced back don't you think?"

"Well, Walt, let me put it this way—" Brent began.

MAGGI SCARCELY KNEW what she was eating. Saunders, strangely quiet that night, served the dinner, then announced that he was retiring to bed just after dessert. Maggi secretly blessed him.

There were a lot of things they had to talk about, a lot of serious things. She had been telling herself that all afternoon. But now, alone with him, her courage began to flag. Her own feelings were too new, too tender, too fresh to risk. Yet, she felt she had to. Several times in the past few days, she had caught him looking at her oddly, particularly after he had watched her fill in for Candace in the skit. Was he, after all, holding her accountable for Jackie's death? Would he ultimately refuse to allow her to address the committee and thus get the revenge he had originally sought?

Ask him now. Make him put his cards on the table.
"Brent, I—"

"It's a beautiful night. Let's have coffee on the terrace."

Did he suspect? Could he read her thoughts in her face? Was he stalling for time? She felt ambivalent emotions, relief over a stay of execution mingled with anxiety. She *had* to know. And yet was afraid to press for an answer.

He slipped his arm around her shoulders and guided her to the terrace. She set her cup down on the glass table just as his lips brushed against her hair. Expectant pulses began to throb along her as their gazes touched. The nettles of desire stung her body as Brent's lips brushed against the side of her neck. He found the area that made lightning flash through her veins. She drew air in short little gasps.

"I've missed you," he told her quietly as he lifted her face to meet his. His kiss was ecstasy as his lips moved slowly, purposefully over hers, drawing her deeper and deeper into a vortex of passion. How was it, she wondered, that no one had ever snatched this man up and run off with him? Could it be that the gods had reserved something so wonderful for her at this stage in her life?

You're getting delirious.

Yes, and I love it.

The sweetness of his mouth excited her further and further. "The coffee's going to get cold," she reminded him. She adored the way he made her aware of every inch of her body.

"Yes, but I'm not." He kissed her again, then rested his forehead against hers. "Do you really want coffee?"

"No."

"Good, neither do I." He drew her up into his arms. "Want to see my Rhett Butler imitation?"

She laughed, delighted with him. "I didn't think you went in for that sort of thing."

"When in Rome . . ." His voice trailed off.

"Anywhere, as long as I'm with you," she breathed happily.

But did she believe that? he couldn't help wondering. No, not now, thinking was for later. He had spent the entire day longing for her. He couldn't let doubts ruin it for him now. Doubts were to be reckoned with tomorrow.

Maggi ran her fingertips along his lips as he carried her into the bedroom. "What makes you smile like that?"

"You." He set her on the floor alongside the bed.

Maggi teased his lips lightly with her own. Once, twice, three times she barely touched his lips, drawing close, then pulling back just before she fell into her own trap.

"No," he said. He began stroking her hair as she attempted to pull back again. "Don't move," he whispered just before he embraced her on a long, sensuous kiss.

Soon her opened blouse fell to the floor and Maggi closed her eyes as she felt his hand slip behind her. The clasp of her bra came undone and the garment loosened. His hands brushed lightly along the sides of her breasts. With slow, sensuous movements, the palms of his hands covered the underswell of her breasts. As he raised them slightly, the bra surrendered to his touch. Maggi did the same.

Maggi almost moaned with anticipation as he lowered his head and kissed each throbbing nipple in turn. His tongue was moist, exciting, caressing.

She wound her fingers through his silky dark head and pressed it closer to her as a low moan escaped her lips. Her fingers relaxed and Brent brought his head up. Cupping her face and tilting her head back gently, he kissed her mouth again. It was a powerful kiss, and yet she sensed that he was still holding back, holding back just enough to bring her excitement and longing to an almost unbearable plateau.

"Clothes can definitely be cumbersome, don't you think?" he whispered against her cheek. The next thing he removed was her skirt, sliding it over her hips and feet.

"If you feel that way," she teased, her pulse throbbing wildly in her throat, "why don't you remove yours?"

The smile he gave her was bewitching. "I seem to be all thumbs."

"You?" The silvery sound of her laughter was muted against the solid dark mahogany furnishings. The moonlight that filtered in through the parted maroon drapes underscored the smoldering look of desire on his face. His wonderful, beautiful face, she thought. She let her fingers roam about the planes of his face. Maggi lovingly memorized each line.

Brent nodded. "It appears I may need your help." His eyes shone with unaccustomed mischief. "Undo me." The words held all the hypnotic power of a siren's song.

His eyes held her fast as she slipped off his tie, sensuously pulling it down and letting it fall from her fingers. Then she stood very, very close and tugged off his jacket and opened the buttons of his shirt, her breasts rubbing against his chest as she moved.

As she pulled the fabric away from his body, Brent made her stop. Maggi's actions were exciting him almost beyond control and he didn't want that to happen. Maggi was to be savored, savored like the brandy he had given her that first night. She mustn't be taken too quickly. "Intermission," he declared, drawing her against him. The gentle sway of his body made Maggi infinitely aware of the soft texture of his chest hair. As his mouth drank in her sweetness, Maggi's grasp of the real world faded even further away.

"Now." His voice was low, deep. "Finish your work now."

Her head was spinning as she went on, tugging the shirt off his broad shoulders. Brent's breathing became a shade more shallow as her cool fingers swept daintily along the contours of his chest, outlining them anew. He felt a new level of desire take hold, a level that almost defied description.

They stood against each other as one from the waist down. His hands rested tightly against her buttocks, pushing her against him, her hips fitting his. Maggi arched her back so as to keep her breasts away from him while she traced small circles with her fingers across his chest. He tried to pull her closer, but she only allowed herself to be pulled close enough so that the very tips of her breasts brushed lightly against his lower chest. Smiling, she swayed gently, massaging the ends of her breasts against him until she felt he was going to burst with desire.

She couldn't believe she was really doing this. She was a temptress and she loved it.

Her pulse raced as he brought her hand to the point where his trousers were joined. The intimate move and its significance brought a throbbing rush of blood to her temples. With fingers that were uncustomarily clumsy, Maggi unhooked his trousers and slid the zipper down. Brent stepped out of them.

"And now," she heard his husky voice say, "we stand as equals." There was a note of teasing in his voice. All that remained between them was a bit of cotton and a hint of silk.

He pulled her against him urgently, the heat of his body sizzling against her own. She was being consumed by the enormous ache she felt, an ache that only he could quell.

His mouth took hers in a searing kiss imprinting his mark on her lips. Somehow, they tumbled back onto the velvet bedspread. The soft texture of the cover hardly registered with Maggi. All she felt, all she tasted, smelled, knew, was Brent. His mouth drained more and more of her, and as it did, she found that she had even more to give, infinitely more.

Brent tucked her against him, fitting her neatly into the pocket formed by his hard body and the bed. His mouth continued devouring hers. His hands stroked her hipline, kneading the curves that were so pliant. After what felt like an eternity, he finally slid his hand beneath the waistband of her underwear, skimming along the perimeter, lowering the boundary lines each time until it clung to only the very essence of her womanhood. Maggi lifted her hips instinctively.

But rather than remove her panties with his hand, his lips moved down to the area, lightly kissing everything that lay in his path. Brent didn't know what possessed him. All he knew was that he had to have her, had to claim every inch of her. She was his as nothing in the world had ever been his before.

Resting the heel of his hand against the base of her undergarment, Brent outlined it with his tongue before he withdrew it from her totally. Feelings exploded inside of Maggi, feelings she never dreamed she had. Another wave of kisses covered the area once blockaded by the tiny bit of silk.

I have met the enemy and I am his. Maggi reversed the thought that had come to her so long ago at his table that first evening. How had she ever thought of making him follow her will? She was pure liquid in his hands.

"And now me."

Maggi blinked and realized that she was looking into his eyes again. The length of his body was once again pressed against hers, and she could feel his pulsating need hot and throbbing.

Brent took her hand, trying to stay his overwhelming desire, and placed her delicate fingertips on his hip. The cotton briefs lay beneath, waiting.

He was waiting.

Reversing their positions, she placed her hand on his chest, making him lie flat. Dropping a pattern of kisses along his hard body, she felt him quiver ever so slightly. It fueled her courage to go on. Mimicking his action and doing her her best to outdo him proved to be torturous ecstasy.

She cast the briefs aside, lowering her lips to recreate the scene he had played only a few moments before. She heard him groan her name. A rush like no other seized her and she pressed her lips closer, reveling in her newfound power.

Maggi felt his hands about her arms, pulling her back to him, pulling her throbbing body along the hardened terrain that waited for her, that wanted her.

"You're a hellcat, Maggi McCree."

He had slipped.

Maggi's eyes grew wide. Was this all—? No, no, it wasn't. It couldn't be. He cared for her. She knew it, felt it.

"Cole," she corrected softly. "Maggi Cole. Your Maggi," she breathed.

"Mine?" He explored the word softly.

"All yours."

It broke the last barrier, the last reserve. Within a moment, she was on her back, with him over her.

There was no time to think, to wonder why he had slipped the way he had. No time to do anything but feel.

And she did. She felt every wonderful, delicious sensation as he parted her legs with his own. The glorious thrust of his arousal sent her sailing to the brink of ecstasy and beyond. He made love to every inch of her, reaching parts of her that she had not known existed.

When they lay spent, sleepy and content in each other's arms, peace enveloped Maggi. She could not remember when she had felt so relaxed, so happy—except for the last time she had been in his arms.

Her fingers splayed out along the soft, downy hairs of Brent's chest beneath her cheek. The rhythm of his breathing brought a lazy smile to her lips, endearing him to her even further. She had no idea why. People thought of silly things when they were in love. And she was.

Maggi drifted off to sleep, smiling.

"OH GOD, I should have gone home," Maggi cried, opening her eyes. Daylight was streaming into the room.

"Why?" Brent asked. "I don't imagine making love is much fun when you do it alone." He pulled her to him. "What's the matter, Maggi?" he asked seriously. He could feel that there was more bothering her than being late, or having her daughters know what they already suspected—that there was a man in their mother's life.

Maggi sat up, pulling the covers around her breasts, resting her head against her knees. She looked at him out of the corner of her eye. He had called her Maggi McCree. She had to know the truth. Was he, after all, just stringing her along? *Now or never.*

But if he kicks you out of bed, you're in a lot of trouble.

Time to play John Wayne instead of Don Knotts.

"It's about the committee meeting."

"Ah, yes, the committee meeting," he said sagely. "The topic that keeps cropping up at the worst times. Right now, my desire is peaking. I don't want to talk business."

He reached for the blanket, but she tugged it back in her direction. "Brent, please, I need to know."

"Know what?"

God, this is hard. "Are you leading me on?"

"If you mean are my intentions honorable—"

"Are you or are you not going to let me talk to the committee?" she asked, interrupting him. She couldn't let him put her off with rhetoric any more. She *had* to come to terms with this.

"Yes."

His direct answer took her aback. It was a full half minute before she asked, "When?"

"Monday."

"Monday!" She stared at him in surprise, her head buzzing. A thousand thoughts ran through it at once. He had told her that the committee was to convene on Monday, but he hadn't even hinted that he was scheduling her to speak to them then.

"Yes, you know, the day so many working people hate. It comes right after Sunday and before Tuesday, sometimes known as Blue Monday—"

He had to stop talking. It is difficult to form words when a woman's mouth is on yours, especially a grateful woman's.

Chapter Fifteen

"Does this mean that you really don't hold me responsible for what happened to Jackie?" Maggi asked breathlessly, in between kissing him.

Brent stopped her and held her at arm's length. "I thought we settled all that. Is that what's been going through your head all this time?"

She nodded. "I was afraid that . . . that . . ."

"That what? That I was going to lead you on, after all? Take advantage of your vulnerable situation, then tell you that the committee had decided not see you? Is that why you're here now, because of the committee?"

"No!" she cried.

"Then why do you think that's why I'm here?" His words weren't angry, merely quiet. There was an undertone of understanding, as if he could see why she would harbor such thoughts.

It made her love him more.

"It's not what I thought of you," she tried to explain. "It's just that I was afraid that you couldn't get rid of the feelings you had about your brother's death. Sometimes the past is hard to bury."

"I don't intend to bury it," he told her. "But neither do I intend to let the past bury me any longer." He kissed her slowly, moving his lips gently over hers. His kiss grew in intensity with each moment. "I have a very promising future, it seems."

She knew he meant the immediate future. Maggi grew warm and pliant, responding to the movements of his body. But just before her mind slipped away totally, his words rang in her mind. "A promising future." Would there be a future for them after the show? He might have forgiven her, but she felt that he would probably never forgive the industry she was so closely involved with. How would that affect their relationship? If he wanted her to give it all up for him, could she feel whole not working anymore?

The same thoughts plagued Brent.

And neither one wanted to let the other see.

They made love as if their very souls depended on it.

"Hi, Mom, have a nice night?" Nikki asked with a broad grin when Maggi walked into her hotel suite several hours later. It was close to ten in the morning.

Maggi looked from Rachel's face to Nikki's. They had always been nothing but honest with one another. The pang of guilt at the kind of example she was setting for them faded quickly. "I had a wonderful evening, thank you." She sank down on the love seat and hugged one of the throw pillows to her. "What would you two like to do today?"

"Have lunch at some exclusive restaurant," Nikki said.

"Where we can pump you for information about our future father," Rachel added with a knowing smile.

Maggi laughed. Were her feelings that obvious? "Well, now, young lady, I think we're counting chickens here," she said, looking at them fondly. Marriage. It seemed so simple to the girls. And wouldn't it be heavenly if...?

No, he hadn't said anything like that. Being allowed to meet with the committee couldn't be equated to getting a proposal. Things had been ironed out between them up to a point. She had to be satisfied with that. *You have to walk before you can run. Usually.*

But that didn't mean she couldn't dream.

"You mean you're just fooling around?" Nikki pretended to be shocked as she narrowed her brows. "Mother, have you given serious thought to the consequences of—?"

Maggi whacked her with the pillow. The words were very familiar. They were part of a long lecture she had given Nikki last year when Nikki had wanted to give in to the demands of a certain high school hunk. "Yes, yes, I have," she answered.

From the way she said it, Nikki knew it was time to drop the subject.

MAGGI FOUND, AS USUAL, that she had little time to spare that weekend for her daughters. Hers wasn't a job she could walk away from on Saturday and Sunday. It followed her around like a shadow. There was a tempest to smooth out before she could manage to leave for lunch with Nikki and Rachel.

Sunday was spent preparing for Monday's presentation. Just because she had an appointment with the committee didn't mean she had its money. She knew she had to make a good presentation. She couldn't afford any slipups. Although she felt her cause was worthy, she also knew that the foundation was besieged daily by scores of "worthy" causes. The foundation more often subsidized research grants or added on to existing medical colleges. Her cause was definitely not the kind it normally reviewed.

"How are you doing?" Norman asked just before she was set to leave for the meeting. It was an exceptionally dreary Monday morning. Maggi hoped it wasn't an omen.

Maggi gave Norman something she hoped would pass for a smile. "As if I'm about to walk my last mile. My butterflies are hatching Concorde jets in my stomach. Nikki," she said, turning to her daughter, "do I look as scared as I feel? No, never mind." She waved away Nikki's answer before the girl had a chance to speak. "I couldn't possibly look as scared as I feel."

Norman put his hands on her shoulders. "Where's the fearless Maggi Cole that I know?"

"In the hotel, cowering under the covers," she cracked. She passed her hand over her face. "Oh, God, if they turn us down..."

"We'll find another way," Norman assured her, giving her a quick squeeze. He had never seen her this nervous before. Was it just the benefit, or did her sudden display of cold feet have something to do with Brent?

"You really believe that?" she asked.

"No." He shrugged. "But it sounds good."

"I can always rely on you in times of strife," she said dryly.

"That's what I'm here for."

Maggi looked at her watch. It was eight o'clock. The meeting was at ten, but she didn't want to take any chances on traffic making her late. "Well," she said, picking up the blueprints, and a vinyl bag with a movie projector in it, "I'm off to see the Wizard."

"Watch out for the Munchkins," Norman warned. "I heard they're all a racy lot." His comment brought the smile he had hoped for.

"Wish me luck," Maggi told them.

"Luck, Mom," Rachel kissed her.

"Knock 'em dead, Mom," Nikki chimed in with a a squeeze of her hand.

"What's that?" Norman wanted to know, nodding at the vinyl bag.

Maggi looked down. "Oh, the movie projector. Last minute insurance."

"You're going to show movies if they get bored?" he asked.

"Just one," she answered. "One I hope gets their attention. It was a sudden inspiration. I had Roxanne ship it in from the studio for me."

"Don't forget the popcorn," Norman called after her as she left. "Well, girls," he said, turning back to Maggi's daughters, "it's time to start praying for the Miracle on Thirty-Fourth Street to move uptown a few blocks."

MAGGI DID A LOT OF PRAYING on her own before the cab arrived at the foundation. As she had surmised, the morning traffic was horrendous, but she had given herself enough leeway to get to her destination with plenty of time to spare. *Just me and my butterflies,* she thought, wishing that she could calm down. This was worse than a case of stage fright. She hadn't felt like this in years, she thought. When she had approached the other donors, she had been cool, calm, collected. She had been nothing if not the picture of confidence.

Now I look like the Picture of Dorian Gray. I've got to calm down. Norman's right. If I don't succeed here, we can still find someone else to back us.

Who are you kidding? Santa Claus is out of town until Christmas. And the Tooth Fairy only leaves quarters.

"Hey, lady, we're here," the cabdriver repeated, turning around to see if the attractive woman he had picked up at the theater had fallen asleep in the back seat.

"Sorry. Just thinking," Maggi explained, leaning forward to pay the fare.

"Dat's my problem, too," the cabdriver remarked, tapping his forehead "Always thinkin'."

Maggi's legs felt as if they were on loan from a papier-mâché factory. They certainly didn't feel as if they were her own or capable of supporting her. She was counting on Brent to give her moral support.

What if he has a change of heart? What if he decided not to vote my way at the last minute? He's known me for only a little while. He's lived with the memory of his brother all his life.

Steady, this is no time to become irrational or get cold feet.

Hefting her vinyl bag over her shoulder like a soldier about to go into battle, Maggi approached the familiar guard and gave him her name. For the first time, she thought, she was going to enter the citadel legally.

"I'm sorry," he said with triumph. "It's not here."

"Not here?" she cried, peering around his stocky shoulder and trying to get a look at his list of people to allow in. "But it has to be. I have an appointment with the committee."

"Look, lady," he said, displaying the plodding, stubborn patience that was the hallmark of his character, "there's no Mrs. Cole here." It pleased him to turn her away. He still held a grudge against her for pulling the wool over his eyes that first time. That, too, was a hallmark of his character.

It didn't look as if the woman was going to go away. He turned back to the list. "I've got Anderson, Hathaway, Danvers, McCree, Shw—"

"McCree?" she echoed, grabbing his arm so hard that he stopped reading.

"Yes. Maggi McCree," he read. "Now—"

"That's me," she told him.

He eyed her suspiciously. "I thought you said Cole."

"I'm both. McCree is my—was my stage name," she said eagerly.

He stared at her for a moment, debating. "Well, Mr. Sommerfield would probably say okay, I guess," he muttered, crestfallen over the lost opportunity to pay her back. "They want us to tighten up security here," the man explained lamely, covering his tail he thought, as he opened the door for her. "There've been some undesirables sneaking in lately."

She didn't realize that his comment was aimed at her. She nodded, barely hearing him. He had slipped again, she thought. Did it mean anything? *Steady, Maggi, you're losing your grip.*

"HELLO, I'M MAGGI COLE," Maggi said to the woman sitting at Marietta's desk. "I have an appointment with the committee at ten." As the woman in the soft, feminine attire began to scan an appointment list, Maggi interjected, "I might be listed as McCree. That was my professional name."

"Professional name?" the woman repeated, her Southern accent making everything a soft melody.

"Yes, I was an actress."

The admission brought immediate interest to the secretary's face. Now, this was more like it, Maggi thought. Brent had hired a human being for a change.

"Oh, yes, right here," Diane said. "Maggi Mc-Cree. You're early."

Why is he using my old name? "Yes, I know," Maggi answered, looking toward Brent's closed door. She had to talk to him. "If Mr. Sommerfield is in, I can wait in his office—"

"No, I'm afraid he's not." The woman appeared to be genuinely sorry.

"He's not in?" Maggi repeated dumbly.

"No, he said he'd be running late this morning. He won't be in until after eleven."

After eleven. After her presentation. *Why isn't he going to be here?* The Concorde jets in her stomach were threatening to crash. *Why* wasn't he here? Did something really come up at the last minute, or was there a deliberate reason for his absence?

"Did he say why he was going to be late?"

Unlike Marietta, Diane didn't appear to be the least bit put off by Maggi's probing. "Oh, no, but I wouldn't think of asking him. I'm new here. It wouldn't do to make waves."

Maggi gave her a feelingless smile of agreement and retreated to a leather sofa on the opposite side of the hall, carrying her blueprints and her projector and feeling suddenly very, very alone.

She told herself she was making mountains out of proverbial molehills. Something had just come up at the last minute and he couldn't come. Maybe he'd still make it back in time, before her presentation.

But he didn't.

"You can go in now, Miss McCree," Diane said, standing over her. Maggi was so deep in thought, she hadn't even heard the secretary approach.

Diane led her down a long, wide corridor resplendent with oil paintings of past members. The Wallaby Medical Research Foundation had been around since the last century and prided itself on its fine tradition.

And, Maggi hoped, its generous heart.

Diane closed the door behind her, leaving Maggi to face a room with a long table and seven men seated around it. The chair at the head of the table was conspicuously empty.

"Hello, I'm Walter Wainwright."

A towering, heavyset man took her hand and pumped it. His deportment encouraged her. He appeared friendly, almost jovial. Maggi tried to relax.

Damn it, where was Brent?

"Mr. Sommerfield's told us all about you."

Maggi thought of Friday night. *Not all, I hope.*

"He's sorry he couldn't be here, but he phoned me early this morning and told me to assure you that you have our undivided attention."

For twenty minutes. That was all the time that had been allotted to her. She had to make this good. "Is there some place I can plug this in?" she asked, nodding at the vinyl bag in her hand.

"What is it?"

"My projector. I'd like to show you a very brief film I brought along."

"Of course, of course." Walter showed her to an outlet on the wall and Maggi made her preparations. The mundane busywork helped to calm her down.

Walter introduced her to each member of the committee, continually referring to her as Maggi McCree. And then the floor was Maggi's.

She did, she thought later, rather well. She gave what she hoped was her most moving performance to date. She presented the committee with an enormous amount of facts and figures as to what the daily costs were for the upkeep of the hospital and the home; then she pointed out how much less expensive it would be to renovate them both. She backed up her words with the blueprints and the kind of rhetoric that businessmen could appreciate.

"And now," she said, carefully rolling up the blueprints and putting them aside, "I'd like you to see something else. If someone could draw the curtains please and turn down the lights?"

The room was geared for visual presentations and in a few seconds all was ready for her movie presentation. Maggi turned on the projector.

To the committee's surprise, a clip from a 1948 costume drama began to roll. The hero, swinging from a masthead, slid down a rope and was about to take a beautiful woman into his arms when the deck came alive with pirates. The committee was treated to several minutes of one of the best orchestrated dueling scenes on film.

"I'm sure most of you recognize this scene, or at least this actor. He's Gilbert Montaigne, who fired most of our imaginations in wonderful adventures like *The Renegade Buccaneer*, *Ships at Sea*, and countless other movies. He was thirty-five when this movie was made. And this," she went on, never changing her tone as another scene merged with the first; the quality was far different and the committee saw the interior of a rest home, "is Mr. Montaigne today."

The contrast was overwhelming and depressing. An old man sat in a wheelchair, staring forlornly out into the distance.

"He had a stroke several years ago," Maggi said quietly. "Not many people know. Long forgotten by the public, he has used up all his savings. There was nowhere for him to turn but the retirement home. As you can see—" the camera panned a wide view of the surrounding area—"it's rather a depressing place in which, for someone like Mr. Montaigne, to live out his final years."

Maggi shut off the projector. Someone turned on the lights. There was an uncomfortable silence in the room.

"Actually, it's rather a depressing place for anyone to spend his existence, but especially these people, who gave us such a wonderful part of themselves, who made us laugh, cry and forget who we were for a few hours while taking our hands and leading us off to another world where anything was possible. I'm asking you now to remember the gifts they gave us." Her voice swelled with emotion. "Remember and give of yourselves now, give the only way it would help. These people desperately need your generous donation.

"The show I propose to put on," she nodded at the list of the cast of stars she had mimeographed for them, "promises to bring in two million dollars. But as you all know, in this world it takes money to make money." She took a deep breath. *This is it* "I still need a quarter of a million to pay off the tremendous bills that the benefit has accrued. The cost of the show would be astronomical were it not for the selfless donations of time and effort given by all those people I've listed. All those people—" she waved at the list "—and a host of people behind the scenes whom I haven't even begun to list. Won't you join them in the effort to make people like Gilbert Montaigne know that we still remember? Remember and are grateful for what they gave us?"

She was finished. It was over. It had taken less time to present than it had to agonize over it. The film had been a stroke of inspiration on her part. Now all she had to hope for was that the men on the committee had all grown up with dreams of being adventurers and pirates instead of playing with Erector sets or fantasizing over Monopoly games. She prayed that they were all moved enough to stretch the medical umbrella to include renovating a hospital that was badly in need of repair.

"Thank you, Miss McCree," Walter said, shaking her hand warmly.

"Cole," Maggi corrected. "I haven't used McCree in over nineteen years."

"Yes, of course; my error. I'm afraid I listed you with the guard that way. Hope it didn't give you any trouble."

Walter Wainwright. *So it was him! Not Brent. All that anxiety for nothing.*

"Tell me," Walter went on, his voice growing just the faintest bit shy, Maggi thought, "what was it like to work with Clark Gable?"

She had at least one vote, she thought with a smile as she began to answer.

WAINWRIGHT HAD PROMISED that the committee would advise her of their decision within a day.

A day. One whole day to agonize over and worry. That had been precisely Norman's reaction as well when she told him how it went. She could see the concern in his face, even though he tried to persuade her that there was nothing to worry about.

But even if they did manage to put on the show despite the mounting debt, the costs would cut into their profit. And the renovation bill was for two million. A small amount, really, when she thought of all that was going to be done. But an insurmountable tab if the amount wasn't collected.

"MAY I COME IN?"

Maggi had just come back from watching a rehearsal and she was particularly exhausted. Her feet ached, she ached and her head was threatening to explode. She turned slowly toward the door.

"Brent!"

Had she more energy, she would have risen to her feet, but she was drained. She stayed where she was. Had he come to tell her that the committee had decided to turn her down?

Why are you such a pessimist suddenly? Must be the weather.

"Where were you today?" she demanded. She hadn't meant for it to sound like an accusation, but it did.

"Business," he answered vaguely, closing the door behind him. "It couldn't be helped." He didn't elaborate any further. "I heard you were quite good. Walter told me you even had a movie for them to watch. He was disappointed that you forgot to bring the popcorn."

"Norman told me I should have," she quipped. *No, don't ask him. No news is good news.* "Any chance of getting an early word on the decision?"

He pretended to consider the question. A small smile was building in the corners of his mouth. "There might be."

Maggi swung her feet down from the other chair and jumped up. She was next to him in an instant, holding on to his jacket. "Well?"

"Not very anxious, are you?" He put his hand into his pocket and drew something out, holding it up with both hands. "How does this look?"

"This" was a cashier's check—a cashier's check for a quarter of a million dollars.

Suddenly Maggi and her tired body parted company. She shed her exhaustion within a blink of an eye, trading it in for elation. "Is this real?" She couldn't believe it!

"The foundation doesn't give rubber checks," he told her, amused at her delight.

"Maggi—" Norman ducked his head in ""—Cunningham wants to run through something new with— Oh, sorry." Seeing Brent in her office, he began to withdraw.

Maggi grabbed his arm before he had a chance to retreat. "No, no, come on in. Come on in and meet the most wonderful messenger we've ever had."

Before Norman could make a comment, appropriate or otherwise, Maggi held up the check before his face. "Feast your eyes on this!"

Norman pushed her hand back to where he could focus in on the amount. He looked from the check to Brent. He had misjudged him all along, he thought in relief. The smile that wreathed his face was one of the largest Maggi had even seen. He shook Brent's hand heartily. "I think this calls for a celebration." He depressed the intercom. "Ethel, send out for champagne."

"What kind of champagne?" came the uncertain voice.

"The best there is," Maggi chimed in. She looked back at Brent. "The very best there is," she repeated, her voice softer.

Chapter Sixteen

As the show drew near, Maggi spent more and more time at the theater. It reached a point where she began losing track of whether it was day or night. Everything was just a continuous whole, flowing toward Friday and the benefit. Demands on her time came from all directions simultaneously. Stars continued arriving almost around the clock. All but Candace Parton.

Maggi saw her daughters far more than she saw Brent. The girls came to rehearsals; when they weren't sight-seeing or shopping, they hung about her office trying to be useful but mainly enjoying being part of the excitement generated by the extravaganza. Brent was hardly more than a voice on the phone.

Maggi was uneasy about how he would tolerate being placed a very distant second, but she didn't have much time to worry about it. There was always something else vying for her attention.

"Never again," she vowed to Brent when she called him the morning of the show. "I feel that I've aged a thousand years."

"I'll have to see that for myself," he told her. She could hear the smile in his voice. *Do you know how much I love you?* she wondered.

"I'm counting on it. Be here tonight?" she asked almost shyly. She never knew that she could miss someone so much. It had been three days since she had felt his arms around her. Three days, two hours and nine minutes to be exact. *A lovesick fool. They write songs that twang about people like you.* "I've got a seat reserved out front if you're interested." She had already sent out tickets to the other members of the board. But his required more of a personal touch, much more. She held her breath, waiting for his answer.

"No, I'll pass it up, thanks."

Maggi felt a freezing emptiness take hold.

"I'd rather be backstage, bothering the producer."

She let out a sigh of relief, not even trying to mask it. "You could never bother the producer. She plans to stick to you like glue."

"Promises, promises."

"Ms. Cole, they need you downstairs," Ethel cried. She was in costume, as she had been all morning. Her part was just that of an escort, leading one of the screen stars of yesterday past an admiring audience, but it was enough for her. She was awe-struck and nervous. Maggi had a suspicion that Ethel had slept in the costume. "It's about your part," she added breathlessly.

"I've got to go now," Maggi told Brent.

"Yes, I heard her," he said quietly. "I'll see you later."

Later, Maggi thought. The word held promise.

IT WAS THE FINAL RUN-THROUGH. Dress rehearsal. Once backstage, Maggi felt the tension and excitement almost overwhelm her. It crackled more intensely than anything she had ever experienced when she was making movies. Or was that because time had muted her memory? She didn't know. All she knew was that she was happy to be part of all this. She had already slipped into her costume in her office and was ready and waiting to go on. She and George Garfield were on right after the opening number.

Halfway through their skit, a loud voice from the back of the auditorium interrupted. "Oh, Maggi, how amusing, dear. But that's my part."

Everything stopped as Maggi squinted past the footlights, trying to see who was talking. Candace Parton, looking unbelievably glamorous in a full-length mink coat that defied the weather, came forward. She mounted the steps on the side and joined the duo onstage.

"You're a little late, Candy," Maggi said tersely. "You were supposed to be here last week."

"Details, details." The woman waved a jewel-laden hand airily. "The point is, I'm here now."

"The point is," Maggi corrected, "the show goes on tonight."

Candace smiled a smile that millions of people had grown to know and clamor for. "I'm well aware of that. Otherwise, I still wouldn't be here." She let her coat fall from her shoulders and handed it carelessly to Maggi. "Thanks for filling in, dear. I'll take it from here."

The director came out of the wings, impatience etched on his face. "There's no time to rehearse."

"Don't insult me. I don't need to rehearse," Candace informed him sweetly. "The part is almost non-existent." Another radiant smile. "Shall we take it from the top?"

Cunningham looked at Maggi, waiting for her to say something. Everyone, she felt, was waiting for her to say something. She was, after all, the producer. It would be very easy to tell Candace that she had been replaced, but Maggi knew that the audience would prefer to see Candace Parton in all her glitter than see a returning child star who hadn't been on the screen for twenty-two years. It was all perfectly clear-cut and logical.

What wasn't was the hollow disappointment that was taking hold.

"You heard the lady, Harold," Maggi said to the director. "Get on with it. I'll have wardrobe get this ready for you," Maggi said, indicating her gown.

Candace blew her a kiss. "You're a dear, Maggi. Do handle the coat with care."

Okay, "dear" Maggi, get yourself out of here before someone reads your face.

Maggi hurried off. She wanted to get out of the outfit and away from the auditorium. She needed air.

Norman frowned from the sidelines as he watched her leave.

"HEY, MOM, what's the matter?" Nikki asked when Maggi walked back into the office. She slid off the desk. "You look awful."

"Comes with the territory," Maggi said, stripping off the mist-blue gown.

"Dress rehearsal over already?" Rachel asked, unaccustomed to seeing her mother upset.

"It is for me." Her daughters looked at her, confused, and she knew that she owed a little more of an explanation than the emotional shorthand she was spouting. "Candace Parton just arrived."

"Candace Parton? Wasn't that her part you were...?" Nikki began.

"It was," Maggi said. "And now she's here to take over." She struggled into her own outfit. Running late, she had thrown on a pair of jeans and a light sweater that morning.

"Be a dear and take this over to wardrobe. Tell them to let out the bodice or Candace will strangle. As for this—" she indicated the mink "—take it out in the alley and set it free," she added sarcastically.

"But she just can't—" Rachel protested.

"Oh, yes, she can." Maggi patted Rachel's cheek, trying to mask her own disappointment in the face of her daughter's. "That's show biz, honey," she quipped. "Besides, Candace claims to be prepared, and the audience would much rather see a star than somebody making a five-minute comeback." She winked, hoping that she was convincing. She certainly didn't feel convincing. She felt lousy. She headed for the door.

"Where are you going?" Rachel asked.

"For a walk," Maggi told her. "Just a walk."

"Want company?" Nikki offered.

The line that gave her away, she knew, was "Not right now." But she couldn't help it. She wanted to be alone for a while, to sort things out, to clear her head and deal with this new emotion that had taken her by surprise.

MAGGI SHOVED HER HANDS into her pockets. It was time to stop feeling sorry for herself and get back. She had no idea how long she had been out. New York streets were always crowded; it was a matter of varying degrees. And she had forgotten to put her watch back on when she had surrendered the diamond bracelet to the nervous-looking security agent. The part had called for diamonds and glitter. *Your part is backstage; not onstage; making sure the security man has nothing to be nervous about.* For the show, they were using over a million dollars' worth of jewels and furs, giving the public everything that went with the make-believe world of Hollywood.

Maggi headed down the back way and threaded through the alley. A ragged derelict stopped her, his hand mutely upturned. Maggi dug deep into her pocket, pulled out a fistful of change and handed it to him. The derelict shuffled away without so much as a word of thanks.

She didn't see the man in the shadows.

"Returning to the scene of the crime?"

"Brent!" she cried. "What are you doing here?"

He took her into his arms. "Nikki called. She said that you had been replaced and were upset."

"And you came?" she marveled. He had left his office in the middle of the day for her. The Brent Sommerfield she had first met would have considered that a sacrilege.

"Looks that way."

Maggi smiled. "Yes, it certainly does." She savored her moment of contentment.

"Nikki's concerned," Brent told her. "And so am I. Are you all right?"

"Perfectly."

Brent looked at her dubiously.

"No, really, I'm fine. I wasn't so fine about an hour or so ago, but I'm okay now. I had a serious talk with myself." She grinned self-deprecatingly. "What time is it, anyway?" she asked suddenly.

"Let's forget about time for a few minutes. Nikki told me that you've been running yourself ragged around the clock." He pulled her over to the doorway, fitting her neatly against himself. "Let's just talk."

Maggi laid her cheek against his chest. "Summit talks like this could lead to world peace." She sighed contentedly, letting herself relax for a moment. "But there's really nothing to talk about. I'm okay." She looked up at him, her eyes shining. "Really, I was just being silly, trying to catch some of the stardust. I thought I missed it all.''

"Thought?"

"Thought," she reiterated. "I don't know how I could have done it, but I forgot how much heartache was attached to acting. Oh, I knew it intellectually," she said. "I dealt with it all the time, on the other side of the camera. But emotionally, I had divorced myself from it. I forgot how very nerve-wracking the uncertainty and the disappointment can all be. That part of my life is over."

She said it as if she had no regrets. And she didn't. She had come to terms with her momentary wave of nostalgia. It was nothing more than an effort to recapture her youth. "It's fun, even thrilling, to hear the applause and see the faces beaming just for you. But then the very next moment, the applause and the smiles are for someone else. What I'm doing is far more fulfilling. Candace Parton could never put together a show like the one I have."

"I don't think anyone could," Brent told her loyally, laying his forehead against hers.

She adored him for humoring her.

"You realize, of course," he said, getting a bit more serious, "that you're ruining my speech."

"Your speech?" she echoed, puzzled.

"Well, you're not the only one who's been doing some soul-searching. I've had a lot of time to think while you've been playing P. T. Barnum."

"And?"

"And," he said quietly, "I've finally licked this feeling I've had about your industry."

Maggi held her breath as she waited expectantly for him to go on.

He ran his hand gently along her cheek. "I've finally put all my old ghosts to bed, or wherever you put ghosts from the past."

"To rest," she prompted.

"Thank you." He smiled at her. Maggi couldn't remember when she had seen a more beautiful smile, Candace Parton and her orthodontist notwithstanding. "To rest," he repeated. "Do you remember Walter Wainwright?"

She nodded. "The man who looks like the Saint Bernard in *Topper*."

"I've never quite thought of him that way." Brent laughed. "But he said something to me the other day that helped put the whole thing into perspective. He remembered you and said something like, isn't it wonderful the way she bounced back? And you did," Brent told her, taking both her hands in his. "You took what life, what the studio, what Hollywood had to throw at you and you bounced back. You *made* something of yourself. You had and have spirit. Something," he went on, "that Jackie lacked."

"I realized that everyone was a bit to blame for what happened to Jackie. But mostly, the blame lay with him, not with you, not with Hollywood. Not even with my mother." A bitter smile twisted his lips. "If he had had half the courage to face up to things the way you had, he'd be here today, maybe doing the same thing that you're doing. Maybe selling shoes. I don't know. But he'd be here. Jackie killed Jackie. No one else did.''

Maggi wrapped her arms around Brent, sealing her body against him. "Oh, Brent." Tears shimmered in her eyes.

"Hush," he said, wiping away a tear as it spilled onto her cheek. "I came here to give you a shoulder to lean on, not to make you cry."

"I don't want your shoulder," she said. "I want all of you."

"You already have that."

Maggi moved to kiss him, but to her surprise he didn't bend into the kiss. Instead, he reached into his pocket and took something out. He pressed it into her hand.

Maggi stared down at the blue velvet box. "What's that?"

"Why don't you open it and see?" he prompted.

She was afraid, afraid of disappointment. In the end, Brent opened it for her. Even in the overcast light of the alley, the diamond solitaire blazed.

"What is this for?" she breathed.

Brent began to laugh. "I thought that everyone in Hollywood knew what a diamond ring was for."

She had to hear him say it. "What?"

He drew her back into his arms. "It's forever," he whispered quietly into her hair.

For a moment, Maggi couldn't see straight. The overwhelming sensations that were racing through her made it impossible to focus on either her surroundings or her thoughts. And then, when she did, the tight hold on reality she had just regained forced her to look at the situation from a a logical standpoint.

"Do you think this is wise?" she asked, her voice husky with emotion.

"Wisest thing I've ever done."

"Brent, I love you." How was she going to say this? "I don't think I've ever loved anyone half as much as I do you."

"There's a 'but' hanging in your voice," he observed. His own voice was filled with understanding. Now that he had conquered the devils of his past, everything else seemed small in comparison. Whatever obstacles she thought she was going to throw his way, he was more than equal to them.

Maggi pressed her lips together. Was she crazy? Was she going to risk losing this wonderful man because of a pattern her life had taken on? But it wasn't just a pattern, she realized. It was a very basic part of her. *Love me, love my life,* she thought cryptically. "There are going to be problems ahead."

"I don't expect a storybook finish—just something bordering on one," he quipped. "Okay," he said gamely, "what problems?"

"My work. I know that this is a terrible time to be thinking of it—"

"Why?" he cut in. "I don't expect you to give up your work. I thought I made that clear."

"Well, you did, but—"

"So?"

He wasn't making it easy. "My work keeps me, predominantly, in California. And yours—"

"... will keep me in California as well."

"What?"

He closed her mouth gently with his finger. "You'll catch flies," he admonished.

I don't understand."

"Let me explain and maybe you will." He grinned. "The foundation has been after me for years to transfer to the California branch. They want me to head up the Los Angeles office. Because of all the bitter memories I harbored, I kept turning them down. But now, there aren't any more bitter memories, only the promise of the future." He kissed her lightly, once, twice, and then again. Maggi stirred against him, rosy with needs and desires that couldn't be accommodated at the moment. "There are only sunshine and rainbows ahead."

"To have rainbows, you're going to need rain."

"Light sprinkles only."

She looked at him skeptically. "You sure you're from California? Out there, when it rains, it *really* rains."

"No," he said quietly, his eyes caressing her face, "I don't remember California. I don't remember anything at all. Except that my life started the day you came into it."

The back door burst open just then and one of Maggi's assistants all but toppled out. "Maggi," he cried breathlessly, "they've been looking all over for you."

"Let them wait a little longer," Maggi said just before she kissed Brent. "I've got something important to do."

Epilogue

The show ran over by thirty-five minutes. Everyone associated with it, especially the audience, wished that it had run over for at least another hour. No one wanted to see it come to an end.

Just before the camera crew stopped taping, Maggi came out from behind the curtain. The lights played off her royal blue gown, catching the silver trim. For a moment, it looked as if she had stars caught in her dress. They were certainly caught in her eyes, Norman thought, watching her. He was proud of her that night, prouder than he had ever been. She had taken an impossible task and had pulled it off with aplomb.

"Taught her everything she knows," he said to Brent, standing at his side. Nikki and Rachel, Norman noticed, were gathered on the man's left. He smiled. They had taken to him already, which was a good thing. Norman had noticed Maggi's diamond the moment she walked back into the auditorium. He could finally stop worrying about her. Things were going to be fine.

"And we've made, because all of you turned out to see all of us," she was telling the audience, "two million—" whistles and stomping accompanied her words—"five hundred and twenty-seven thousand—give or take a dollar."

The audience clapped and laughed in response to her words.

"Think she's finally licked it?" Norman felt it safe to ask Brent. They both knew what he was referring to.

"No," Brent said thoughtfully. "I think it's something that stays in your blood, a little like a disease. But she knows how to handle it, and that's the main thing."

Maggi melted back, a wave of cheers and applause accompanying her as she appeared backstage.

"Well," she said happily, looking at Brent more than anyone. "It's over."

"No," he told her, taking her hand, "it's just beginning."

The thrill in her heart told her that he was right.

Harlequin American Romance

COMING NEXT MONTH

#149 SPECIAL DELIVERY by Judith Arnold

They had first met on a Connecticut beach—but what they'd shared transcended friendship. For on that foggy beach Roberta's baby demanded to be born and Kyle, a total stranger, had helped deliver her. They had not seen each other since, but now, five years to the day, they are to meet again.

#150 FOREVER IS A LONG TIME by Pamela Browning

It was a long way from the North Carolina mountains to Hollywood, but in two years Sharon Ott had become a singing star and learned enough about the world to know what Brad Fielding wanted. This was one move she would have to decide by pure instinct. And her instinct warned her not to trust Brad.

#151 ANGEL'S WALK by Kathleen Carrol

Angel's Walk meant everything to Suzanna. She would never leave the heirloom house. If it was in danger, then she was, too. The new engineer was their only hope. Didn't Cam Harris create lakes and divert rivers every day of the week? Suzanna held tight as Cam swept into town, into her life and finally into her heart. And she waited for a miracle.

#152 SNOWBIRD by Beverly Sommers

Loud, lawless and unlivable—that was Alyce's Alley. At least it should have seemed that way to Patty, a transplanted Boston highbrow. Mike couldn't understand why she stayed. She was too ornery to be a spy, and despite rumors, he didn't think she was crazy. He only knew she made his life miserable. But then why didn't he want her to leave.

Take 4 best-selling love stories FREE
Plus get a FREE surprise gift!

WHAT READERS SAY ABOUT HARLEQUIN INTRIGUE ...

Fantastic! I am looking forward to reading other Intrigue books.

*P.W.O., Anderson, SC

This is the first Harlequin Intrigue I have read ... I'm hooked.

*C.M., Toledo, OH

I really like the suspense ... the twists and turns of the plot.

*L.E.L., Minneapolis, MN

I'm really enjoying your Harlequin Intrigue line ... mystery and suspense mixed with a good love story.

*B.M., Denton, TX